Penguin Books
A Suitable Case for Corruption

Norman Lewis has written twelve novels and five non-fiction works. *A Dragon Apparent* and *Golden Earth* are considered classics of travel, and *Naples '44* has been described as one of the ten outstanding books about the Second World War. His novel *The Sicilian Specialist*, based on at that time undisclosed facts about the Kennedy assassination, was removed from sale in some American cities following a Mafia ban. Lewis travels extensively and as far as possible off the beaten track in search of inspiration for his work. Apart from writing books his main interest lies in the study of the cultures of so-called primitive peoples. He regards as his principal achievement the world reaction to an article written by him entitled 'Genocide in Brazil', published in the *Sunday Times* in 1968. This account, after a long personal investigation, of the near-extermination of the Indians of that country led to a change in the Brazilian law relating to the treatment of Indians, and the formation of organizations such as Survival International, dedicated to the protection of aboriginal people.

Norman Lewis lives with his family in Essex.

Norman Lewis

A Suitable Case for Corruption

Penguin Books

Penguin Books Ltd, Harmondsworth, Middlesex, England
Viking Penguin Inc., 40 West 23rd Street, New York, New York 10010, U.S.A.
Penguin Books Australia Ltd, Ringwood, Victoria, Australia
Penguin Books Canada Limited, 2801 John Street, Markham, Ontario, Canada L3R 1B4
Penguin Books (N.Z.) Ltd, 182–190 Wairau Road, Auckland 10, New Zealand

First published by Hamish Hamilton, 1984
Published in Penguin Books 1986

Printed and bound in Great Britain by
Cox & Wyman Ltd, Reading
Typeset in Linotron Stempel Garamond

To Les, with so many thanks
for all the work

Chapter One

Cairo, proffering indifferently either astonishment or delight, left the Secretary of State depressed. It was a city that reminded him of an aged, wrinkled face, lost to both beauty and to hope. Inspired by a morning full of grace, a man in the street might have raised his eyes to a vision of minarets lifted gently in sashes of mist that would shortly replace them on their shafts. But the narrow view from the windows of the great embassy car, wriggling like a centipede through streets that seemed about to close in and trap them, was crammed with disturbing, sometimes repellent detail. The Secretary of State saw stained walls, butchered animals hung up to bleed on the sidewalk, scabs and spittle, and donkey droppings on the road, and he could feel malevolent staring eyes behind trellised shutters. There were even cows astray in the roaring traffic lanes of Tahrir Street and there was something shocking in the sight.

'Would you look at that?' he said to the Ambassador who had come to meet him, but who remained unperturbed by such spectacles. 'Goddam cattle in the main street, huh?' The cows were browsing off a bale of tobacco that had fallen from a truck, being buffeted as they munched by the fenders of passing cars.

'Some guy told me they have one million people living in a cemetery in this town,' the Secretary of State said. 'I believe they do,' the Ambassador said. 'I believe they do.'

They had become separated from the car with the bodyguards in the iron avalanche of vehicles sliding down Tahrir Street towards the Nile. This worried the Ambassador who told the driver to turn off the agreed route and take a short cut to the Embassy in the Garden City. It proved a mistake. Here in a mud-rutted alleyway they were held up as a result of an accident in which a man had been run down and killed. The corpse had to be left where it lay for the arrival of the police and the people of the street had torn branches from a tree to make a bed for it in the middle of the road. The two men got out and the Secretary of State, standing with the Ambassador found himself staring down into a face embowered in leaves, and into open eyes retaining only the slightest expression of concern. It was an experience that disconcerted him, as did the routine screech of the professional mourning women someone had rushed to fetch. Suddenly he was tired.

He led the way back to the car. There was sweat in his eyes and grit under his teeth, and the city's noises seemed to be rattling round in his brain. Too many changes of scene, he thought, too many hours on a plane, and then at the end of it all, this hellhole where his showdown with Parsons, Middle Eastern head of the Agency, would shortly take place.

The Ambassador remained imperturbable, ignoring even the great braying of car-horns that had started at their back. 'You'll see Pharaoh in the morning?' he asked.

'That's what I plan to do. Tell him once again what a great man he is.'

'His megalomania's worse. It's become an irreversible condition.'

'I know, but we need him. That's why I'm back, and that's why I'm going to fire Parsons if I have to.'

'Do you believe this assassination rumour?'

'It's no rumour, make no mistake about that. This is a situation Parsons should have handled, but he can't. He's fallen down on his job. What can I do to this guy short of firing him?'

'Tell him you'll pull him out. Threaten to recall him to Washington,' the Ambassador suggested.

'I'm talking about punishment, not promotion.'

'He's been here a long time and he likes it. Collects antiques. Very active in the Southern Baptist movement in the community. He wants to stay.'

'What, here, for Christ's sake?' The Secretary of State could hardly believe his ears. 'Do *you* want to stay here, Bill?'

The Ambassador smiled enigmatically, and a blind man with grey pebbles for eyes and chewing at a grilled sparrow on a skewer rapped at the window, then cupped his hand. The driver, a Nubian giant, had gone running to the rear to investigate the chances of reversing out. Scolded and blamed for the hold-up, he now returned with a cluster of angry men hanging like bats from his wide sleeves. Taking his seat again, he engaged gear and they nudged forward, mounting the sidewalk to avoid the wide death-bed of branches, crunching through a sierra of compacted garbage, upsetting a vegetable stall. Howls of execration followed them as they crashed back into the roadway again and picked up speed.

'We lead rather a sheltered existence at the Embassy,' the Ambassador said. 'I'm sure Parsons does too in his way. It might be worthwhile to tell him you're thinking of moving him and test his reaction. If you fire him, who are you going to find to put in his place?'

'Exactly. Who?'

After his working lunch at the Embassy the Secretary of State summoned Parsons into his presence. His face was creased with mock benignity. 'Henry, something I just heard surprised me. I was told you like it here.'

'It's a reasonably satisfactory posting, Mr Secretary.' Chilled by the Secretary's teasing manner and the presence of a smile habitually used to express displeasure, Parsons fumbled among his thoughts. 'It's not so much the physical environment, Mr Secretary. It's the work environment that counts.'

'The work environment. Sure. And that's good, I gather.'

'It's satisfactory.'

'Must help to be able to speak the language?'

'It's essential.'

'Where would you be in a place like this if you didn't?' The man was even beginning to look like a gippo, the Secretary of State thought, with the kind of face you saw all the time around the bazaar, eyes pulled together from squinting at scarabs looted from tombs.

The Secretary of State came to the point. 'Do you know why I'm here?'

'I assumed it was about the report on the President.'

'You assumed right. Know something, Henry? That report got me out of a warm bed at six in the morning to grab a plane and come out here. I've dragged my ass half across the world to talk to you about it. And I want to know what action has been taken.'

'We passed the information to the Egyptian security services.'

'That's all—then you sat on your hands?'

'This is the laid-down procedure, Mr Secretary. I don't see what else we could have done.'

'You uncovered a plot to kill the President and then all you did was throw it in the Egyptians' lap. And what are *they* doing about it?'

'They have a contingency plan which includes increasing the size of the presidential escort and the number of guards at Giza, Abu Kom, Bourg el Arab and all the other residences he uses.'

'And you think that's enough?'

'No, I don't, but with all due respect I don't think you appreciate the magnitude of the problem involved. We're dealing with a man who's unrealistic. What are you going to do about a guy who sincerely believes bullets would bounce off him? When we gave him that armoured helicopter, what did he say? His actual words were, "This is a toy I shall never play with. I do not need to defend myself from my children."'

A certain reassuring sternness had returned to the Secretary of State's face. Parsons took heart. 'He lives in a dream world,' he said. 'He tells you, "Every Egyptian is a member of my family. What binds us together is love." His own brother would whack him out if he had half a chance.'

'What you're trying to say is that you can't provide full protection.'

'Only God can provide that, Mr Secretary.'

'Okay, then, the protection a man in his position is entitled to expect.'

'He lost all his friends at Camp David. We can't build a wall round him. A Turk called Aziz runs the security. He's good, but he can't perform the impossible.'

'Henry, whatever it costs us, whatever happens, this man has to be kept alive. Do you know why?'

'I believe you regard him as a kind of insurance against the nuclear holocaust.'

'Right. Because by splitting up the Arab front, which would be irresistible if united, he gave us the present tensional equipoise.'

'It was a smart move, but he's deteriorated since then.'

'If he goes,' the Secretary of State said, 'the Arabs will eventually and inevitably gravitate together once again, and what do you suppose this will lead to?'

'Armageddon,' Parsons said devoutly.

'The final conflict because, if he has to, the Bullfrog will use the bomb. Henry, I have to make you understand. If there's a Third World War, it's right here in the Middle East it's going to start, and there's no conceivable action to stop that happening that isn't justified. You know as well as I do who's at the back of this. The Gadfly.'

'Sure, the Gadfly, as ever.'

'Well, what are we doing about him?'

'Making life hard for him in every way we can.'

'It's not enough. I don't want to tinker with this problem any longer. I'm calling on you for rapid, temperate and pre-considered action to remove the Libyan threat to peace and stability.'

'You mean you want him destabilized?' Parsons suppressed all indications of eagerness or excitement. The chance to set up the processes of destabilization only happened once in a lifetime.

'Call it what you like.' The Secretary of State disapproved

of euphemisms invented by his predecessors. 'What are the feasibilities of setting up an action?'

'Gadfly is the only guy in the world with more enemies than Pharaoh. We can throw him to the dogs any time you want.'

'I want you to do just that. But keep it simple. Beautifully simple. We've suffered from too much complexity in the past.'

The Agency, the Secretary of State decided, was staffed largely by romantics, adventure-loving boys handicapped by their profession in the process of growing up. He recalled his incredulity at the farcical nature of some of the operations reported to him, and even reported in the press. There had been the poison-saturated wet-suit presented to the Cuban Premier; in addition, in the event of that failing to work, the sea-bed where he was wont to snorkel had been planted with explosive shells. 'These complicated set-ups never work,' he said. 'I hate failures. Three out of four of these actions go down the tubes.'

'Due to inadequate planning,' Parsons said. 'We learn from our errors.'

'Well, that's good to know, because if it turns out that we haven't, you're finished, Henry. I noticed from the form you filled out at the beginning of this tour of duty that you put Central America at the bottom of your choice list. Let me tell you now, I'm thinking of sending you to Guatemala. I don't know how you feel about that. They tell me it's a beautiful place.'

'I'd prefer to stay where I am, Mr Secretary.'

'I'm sure you would. But just bear it in mind. Above all I want no evidence of involvement, huh? By which I mean no cans of jam made in Milwaukee left lying around. This has to look like just another native vendetta.'

'You can rely on me, Mr Secretary.'

Before calling his assistant Eddie Brandsteller, Parsons reassured himself by a muttered scriptural passage: *Total submission is due to your superiors for God has raised them to power over you.* Romans thirteen, one. The formula shifted responsibility for whatever might follow him from his own shoulders and left his conscience clear. In a moment Brandsteller stood before him.

'Well, we finally got the green light on the Gadfly,' Parsons said. 'We can go ahead and set up a package. What's the name of that Libyan defector you have on ice?'

'Hawi. Ibrahim Hawi,' Brandsteller said.

'How do you rate him?'

'I'd say he's playing straight. He has reason to. The revolution left him with his jock-strap and his boots. We have quite a file.'

'I'm sure you have, Eddie. Don't tell me about the guy's blood group.' Brandsteller was famous for his collection of information, sometimes carried to absurd lengths. Now Parsons tried to copy the Secretary of State's style of patronising banter, but failed to sound convincing. He was a serious man and people took him seriously. 'I want to know about his background. Is he solid? Does he cast a shadow?'

Brandsteller shot out of the room and came back with a paper typed in single spacing. 'This country has one thousand, one hundred and forty-two Libyan political defectors, most of whom regard Hawi as their leader. He also had a following in his own country. To give you a few names—'

'Never mind about that right now. What was the proposition?'

'He wanted us to organize a small party of headhunters and provide a suitable boat.'

'Let me tell you what comes next,' Parsons said. 'They would make their landing, half of them would go to the Palace and take the Brother Leader out, and the rest would grab the broadcasting station and announce a change of regime. It sounds so easy, doesn't it? Where would they land?'

'I have a map of the town with all the possibilities marked. Want me to get it?'

'Not now. Do you happen to recall how far the nearest

possibility was from the Palace?'

'Seven point eight miles.'

'Seven point eight miles? For Christ's sake, Eddie, doesn't it occur to you to ask how they'd get there?'

'On foot, I guess.'

'Carrying all the usual gear, of course. Eighty, maybe a hundred pounds per man.'

'They could grab any cars that happened to be around.'

'At four or five in the morning. Sometimes I wonder about you, Eddie. Weren't you in the Teheran fiasco?'

'I was remotely associated with it, Mr Parsons.'

'Whatever really happened, there's a question mark hanging over the name of any man who had his finger in that pot of glue. No benefit of the doubt on this one. The slightest slip-up and you'll be out of here. Know what they'll do? Send you to some shit-hole like Guatemala.'

Brandsteller winced. 'You didn't ask me for my opinion.'

'And what is it?'

'Eight miles is too far to walk any time of day.'

'I'm glad we're in agreement,' Parsons said. 'The last thing we want is to take another beating. Why don't you gather the team together and explore the feasibilities. Maybe we can use Hawi. Maybe there's some way we can get round the obvious difficulties, but I'm pessimistic. Anyway, you boys go into it, and come back to me as soon as you can.'

Parsons' meeting with the President did nothing to ease his forebodings. The President, dressed as if to review his troops, launched into a rambling discourse lasting half an hour on the grandeurs of the ancient Kingdom, before Parsons could persuade him to listen to what he had to say and obtain his somewhat tepid approval for the project.

'How was he?' Brandsteller asked.

'As bad as usual,' Parsons said. 'Every time he sees himself on the cover of *Time* magazine he gets worse, and it's happened five times.'

'A firm in London that runs a waxworks museum did a model of him to put on show,' Brandsteller said, 'and he ordered a second one to be sent to his tailors some place like Piccadilly. That's the way they fit his uniform. The face is perfect from the photographs he sent. They cover it with a flag at night.'

'He's fallen victim to the sin of pride. When I told him his life was threatened, he laughed and gave me a chunk of the Koran. "No man can live an hour more than his appointed span", etcetera. The trouble is, if this is to be done at all he's fixed a precise date for it. It has to be the sixth of next month.'

'For Chrissake, why?' Brandsteller asked.

'He has an ul'ema who acts as his guru, who told him it would be a lucky day.'

'What does that give us, two weeks? It's impossible. We may as well forget about it.'

'We can't,' Parsons said.

'I'm going to have to set this up, and I tell you there isn't time. It can't be done.'

'It must be done,' Parsons told him. 'The Secretary of State wants action and he's going to have it. If the President fixes a date that's too soon, that's just too bad. Nothing you or I say is ever going to make him change his mind. We have to do what we can, and hope for the best.'

All that could be discovered of Ibrahim Hawi's life and attitudes bolstered the Agency's confidence, but as a matter of iron routine he was kept under surveillance in all his comings and goings in Cairo. The Arab agent thus employed noted that he spent more time than most praying in one or other of the city's many mosques. However, in the sincere belief in a man's right to his privacy on such occasions, he had left Hawi to himself, slipped away for a mint tea, and been back at the door of the mosque a few minutes later, therefore remaining unaware of Hawi's meeting with the ul'ema who had become the President's adviser and confidant: an encounter, when, following the warmest of embraces, certain secret matters were discussed.

As it was, Hawi passed all the many tests, the order was given for Brandsteller's project to receive provisional covert support, and tentative planning began. It was still hoped that the President might be induced to change his mind and put back the operation's date. A boat was made ready that was radar-equipped and faster and better armed than any comparable vessel afloat—although it had to be admitted that it was bound to advertise its presence wherever it went. According to an outline plan full of unsolved queries, Hawi would probably slip back across the frontier at the beginning of October, and alert his supporters to the imminence of a coup. He would hold himself, and enough vehicles to carry the raiders to their destination, in readiness on the night of the fifth of October for the radio signal that the landing had taken place.

Parsons remained cautious. 'Let's go over the previous actions and ask ourselves why they didn't work. How about the fellows they put ashore from the submarine?'

'It was the middle of the night,' Brandsteller said. 'They got wet, and lit a fire to dry themselves.' He shrugged hopelessly.

'What about that parachute attempt?'

'One guy dropped into the sea, and another came down in an old car dump and broke his legs. The rest of them lost their bearings, wandered around fighting off the dogs till dawn, then turned themselves in.'

'And the disaffected officers?'

'They had no following. Only out to grab anything they could for themselves. They were put up against the wall.'

'A landing by sea has less to go wrong, and you can be surer of delivering a big blow in the right place,' Parsons said. 'Against that is the Russian radar the Gadfly uses, which is better than ours. They'll pick up the ship as soon as its profile clears the horizon. Also where's the landing to be? We still don't know. So far only the long walk is out. Oh for another week, another month.'

His pessimism had transformed itself into a physical

symptom that felt like indigestion. 'Let's even suppose we go ahead with this thing in its present form. Who's going on the party?'

'We're hoping Bullfrog would oblige with a few of Haddad's leg-breakers,' Brandsteller said. 'I don't know how you feel about that. They'll take the canaries out of their cages and twist their heads off.'

Parsons was ready with the Bible. 'St Paul tells us to do evil that good may come.'

'The Turk Aziz would keep them under control. Anyone steps out of line, he'd crack his skull.'

'Just a minute,' Parsons said. 'What's gone wrong here? I talked to this man only yesterday and it was agreed that from now on he's never going to let Pharaoh out of his sight. He said he'd sleep across the door of his bedroom if I thought it was necessary.'

'He told me that too, but the President wants him to go all the same. This is the guy who master-minded the Canal crossing in the Yom Kippur war and he's the only man Pharaoh has confidence in.'

'I don't like it. This could be something that guru of his put into his head. I want Aziz to stay right here where he is.'

'Maybe you can make Pharaoh change his mind, Mr Parsons. I can't see that happening though.'

'I can't either, and my instinct would be to pull out of this, but we can't. A package has to be set up, but the way things are right now it's a step in the dark. I could name ten reasons for you why Teheran went wrong. This has to be foolproof.'

'What would you suggest, Mr Parsons? I'd like to benefit from your experience.'

'If we have to make a landing from the sea it has to be within minutes of the target. We need to know where that can be done.'

'I can go back and talk to Hawi.'

'Hawi has been away too long. These things change all the time. Anyhow, what can a politician tell us about defences?'

'We have aerial photographs,' Brandsteller said. 'The whole area was re-photographed only three months back. About

'12,000 separate shots were taken.'

'Oh sure, and they can pick out a golf-ball at 50,000 feet. What they can't pick out is a mine buried under four inches of sand. The only answer to this problem is to establish contact with someone on the spot.'

'It won't be easy,' Brandsteller said.

'It'll be very difficult, Eddie. These things, as we both know, always are. But that's what you're going to have to do. And remember I don't like that boat. We have to give up the idea of the landing if we can't do better than that.'

'The Secretary of State told you to keep it simple, and nothing could be more simple than a landing. If you could get it right.'

Brandsteller set to work again. About a third of the material stuffing the files of intelligence organizations—the bread and butter of the profession—had been painstakingly extracted from published matter; and Brandsteller, understanding this, kept a team of foreign language experts busy studying and analysing reports in the world press. Only three days after their new task had been assigned, a solution to at least part of his problem was suggested by an item in a French newspaper stumbled on by a member of the team.

Next morning a translation from *Le Monde* was on Parsons' desk. He read:

A Five Year Plan for Libyan Tourism

An announcement that Libya is to inaugurate a Five Year Plan for tourism was made here today by the Board of Tourism and Fairs. While no one expects Tripoli to become the Las Vegas of North Africa in the foreseeable future, the view here is growing that a healthy tourist industry might provide a useful boost to the economy when—as has recently been the case—oil revenues begin to flag. Libya likes to do things in a big way, and the new venture should be taken seriously. As a first step an excellent beach somewhere in or near the Capital itself is to be turned into a Lido, Libyan-style.

For an excessively security-conscious country that has shown nervousness of the possibility of attack by its powerful neighbour to the East, only averted, we are informed, by US veto, this hint of détente is significant.

Parsons put down the sheet and rang for Brandsteller. 'There may be something in this for you,' he said.

'That's the way I feel,' Brandsteller said.

'I want you to find out all you can about whoever it is wrote this. Keep it to three hundred words. I don't want to know about his bridge-work, or if he walks with a limp.'

'It's already been attended to,' Brandsteller said. 'It was all in the computer.' He handed Parsons a second sheet.

Ronald Kemp, aged 43. Born London. Journalist. Married. Wife in England and two sons at school there. Degree in Languages, Leeds University. Studied Arabic at SOAS. Worked as reporter *Leeds Examiner* 4 years. Later correspondent Reuters, France Presse and others. Paris 5 years, Cairo 2 years, Beirut 2 years, Tripoli 4 years. Many short visits to Arab countries: Syria, Morocco, Tunisia. Currently stringer for *Le Monde* and *The Times* as well as agency correspondent and engaged as production consultant for Government English-language publication *The Green Standard*. Kemp has no known political affiliations, and no international communist contacts. Regarded as ambitious, but over-susceptible to feminine charm. Lives well. Some financial instability is demonstrated through cost of establishment maintained in England, and fees estimated at £9,000 per annum for sons' education at leading British school. While not overtly pro-Arab he appears to enjoy the confidence of the regime to a remarkable degree, and this may have aided him to come into the possession of information not available from other sources. Considered reliable and exceptionally accurate in his reporting, was responsible for sensational account of the

OTRAG Company's secret operations—probably leading to their withdrawal—and the news of the installation of SS 12 missiles at Tobruk.

'This,' said Parsons, 'is a guy we have to talk to.'

Chapter Two

Teddy Vickers of the newsagency rang Kemp from London, the telephone jarring harshly in the vast emptiness of the villa. 'Ronald, those last two pieces were really great. How did you dig out all that stuff about OTRAG? We're speechless with admiration. I'm ringing because James Jimson who's a friend of ours wants very much to meet you.'

'If he's thinking of coming here it'll take him up to three months to get a visa.'

'He lives in Malta and for one reason or another it wouldn't be convenient for him to visit you where you are. We'd very much like you two to get together. Would there be any hope of your being able to pop over there for a quick trip?'

'The fare's seventy pounds, each way,' Kemp said, 'and the exit and re-entry visa usually takes time.'

'Nobody expects you to be out of pocket, you know that, old boy. Naturally you'd put in your chit in the usual way. I really do hope something can be done to get you two together. You'd enjoy meeting Jimson. Find you have a lot in common, besides which he's a man who's useful to us and could probably be useful to you in a number of ways. You can get him any time at the Hotel Portugal, Valetta. I'll give you the number. He'll be there any day this week.'

Vickers was self-educated, of working-class origin, with a quick pride and, in Kemp's opinion at their first meeting, secretive and cold. However they had got on well enough in the eight years of their collaboration. 'I have many acquaintances, but few friends,' Vickers often said, but for all that they became friends, and saw a good deal of each other when Kemp was in England. Claire, who was hard to please, liked Vickers. Most people did, although it was easy to see he

15

rarely returned their esteem. If they were useful to him, that was enough. Jimson was useful, and Vickers wanted Kemp to meet Jimson and, thinking it over, Kemp didn't see why he shouldn't. A quick visit to Malta, all expenses paid, would make a pleasant break. He used his connections to by-pass the worst of the exit and re-entry rigmarole and rang Jimson to tell him he would be arriving two days later. He took the Air Malta flight, touched down at four, and had checked in at the pleasantly old-fashioned Hotel Portugal by five.

The telephone in his room rang immediately to say that Mr Jimson was waiting for him in the bar. He proved to be a man of about forty with a deep beach tan and a dense beard. Kemp noticed, as he had observed before in heavily bearded men, that such part of the features as remained in view was extremely expressive, and in this case suggested a geniality which might or might not really exist. 'Feel like a sharpener so early in the day?' Jimson asked. 'Scotch, something of the kind?'

'That would be a very good idea.'

He ordered a double scotch and soda, and Jimson, sipping a tonic water, watched him with twinkling interest. 'Not too much of that back where you come from,' Jimson said. Kemp caught a trace of an American accent, of the kind that sometimes colonized the speech of a much-travelled Englishman of humble origin.

'You can get all the scotch you want,' he said, 'if you're prepared to pay for it, and know the right people. Otherwise you drink something called flash. It attacks the lining of the stomach, fuddles the brain and shortens the life.'

They both laughed. 'It's a nice evening,' Jimson said, 'why don't we walk across to the Barraka Gardens and have a chat? Air-conditioning doesn't seem to be working too well in here.'

The gardens, built on a lofty eminence over the town, were only a hundred yards up the road, and they walked there in a matter of minutes. It was a secluded spot. Kemp knew it well, and was familiar with the local customs at this time, just before sundown, when loving couples went there and the population as a whole stayed away. At the moment of their arrival, although the Barraka was still bathed in evening light, each of its many ornate stone benches was occupied by boy and a girl, well separated from each other, who would fall into each other's arms when the angelus rang to announce the official advent of night.

Kemp and Jimson stood together at the parapet, looking down on the ramparts and bastions of the great city spread out beneath, the innumerable basilicas and churches, the temples and leafy squares over which Christendom had unfurled its standards against the Turks. 'I come here whenever I can to recharge my batteries,' Jimson said. 'I feel renewed by the peace and the tranquillity of the place. Environment plays a great part in my life.'

The angelus clanked sweetly in a nearby belfry; the lights came on all over the town beneath, and the lovers turned to take each other in their embrace. By common consent it was now night, and Jimson seemed to take this as a signal to plunge into the matter in hand.

'Teddy Vickers told you of our interest in your work?'

'He did.'

'I should explain who we are. I represent Agence Presse Libre. We're located in Geneva. Vickers will vouch for our respectability and solvency. We're very impressed by your reports from Libya. Particularly the OTRAG report, which was a marvellous piece of detection. Also, of course, your coverage of Uganda. I can't think how you do so well.'

There was something faintly patronising about this man, a hinted assumption that Kemp was bound to share his views and prejudices which Kemp found irritating, and it prompted him to return short answers. 'I do my best to know all the people who count.'

'That must be the answer. How on earth did you find out about the missiles at Tobruk?'

'I was shown them. The sites, anyway.'

'Perhaps they actually wanted the world to know what was going on.'

'They probably did.'

'Did you put out that report about the assassination attempt on the Colonel last March?'

'What I said was that there had been an alleged attempt. It was never confirmed.'

'But it happened all the same, eh? Who was behind it, the Israelis?'

'Not this time. Some of his officers were disaffected over the Chad affair, and one of them took a pot-shot at him. Nicked him in the chin.'

'What were his guards doing?'

'There weren't any. There rarely are. This man is an Arab. He believes that no man goes before his time has come.'

Jimson shook his head knowingly. 'Fatalism,' he said. 'Something they drink in with their mothers' milk.'

'He likes to relax with his family in the evening. Put his feet up in front of the television. I believe that was when it happened.'

'Relaxes with his family, does he? That's very interesting.' Jimson's hand had fallen on Kemp's shoulder, and he steered him along the parapet into a deeper twilight under the branches of a flowering tree. 'We'd like you to work for us,' he said.

'I'm afraid that's out of the question. I'm under contract.'

'I've been into all that,' Jimson said. 'It wouldn't have been sensible to ask you to come here otherwise. I happen to know we could work out a satisfactory arrangement with your present employers, and that they'd have no objection. We pay very well.'

'For what?' Kemp asked.

'Informative material of all kinds, just as any agency does. I understand from Teddy Vickers that you read Arabic. We'd be interested in having you go through the newspapers and keeping us in the picture about anything new that happens to be going on.'

'It's a tall order. They have newspapers by the dozen full of articles about baby foods, and how to grow tomatoes in water. The paper I do some work for just ran a piece on the place of body deodorants in modern Arab society.'

Jimson guffawed shortly. Kemp had a feeling that constant bubbling derision was concealed by the dense facial hair. 'You'll have to be more specific,' he said.

'This is something we'd like to leave to you, Ronald. Anything that really captures your interest is bound to interest us. That piece you sent in last week on that five-year-plan for tourism, for instance. You made some mention of a beach resort they're going to develop. Now there we seem to have a breakthrough. It's an interesting indication of the way things are shaping. We'd like to know more about that.'

'I can't see there's going to be much more to say. Bathing beaches aren't part of the Arab scene. They can't drink the sea and they can't wash in it, so what's the point? To keep the foreigners pleased they'll probably import a few fancy rocks from Japan and put in some trees in containers which will die when nobody remembers to water them. They might throw in half a dozen moulting flamingoes, with their legs hobbled the way they do with their cows. You'll still have to climb round wrecked cars and empty oil drums to get to the sand.'

Jimson's shoulders shook in a convulsion of hidden laughter. 'Christ, what a place. And where is all this going to happen if it happens?'

'Your guess is as good as mine. It has to be within range of the big hotels they're putting up. I doubt if they've decided on the site.'

'Would that be something you could find out?'

'Possibly.'

'How soon?'

'No way of telling. Whenever they make up their minds, which should be fairly soon. When our Libyan friends decide to do something they don't let the grass grow under their feet.'

'Ronald, from what Teddy tells me you're a man who appreciates straight talk and a clear-cut proposition. I'm not going to beat about the bush. We—that is to say the people I work for—would offer five grand, cash, for the precise location of that beach, providing you can supply it within fifteen days.'

'I don't understand,' Kemp said. 'Why should you want to pay me so much money when the official announcement is sure to be made within the month? It'll tell you all you want to know.'

'We don't want to wait,' Jimson said. 'We can't wait, if you like. That's just the point.' He had dropped his voice, quite unnecessarily considering the utter absorption of every human being within a hundred yards in intensely private affairs. And though his eyes had fallen into dark shadow, Kemp realized that they were fixed upon him intently, as if in an attempt to transmit messages too delicate for words. 'This is a matter of rather special urgency,' Jimson said. 'Need I say more?'

Kemp, under his outward calm, shied like a horse. 'Just a moment, aren't we getting onto rather dangerous ground at this point?'

Jimson's voice, charged with gentle reproof, recovered its vigour. 'Dangerous ground? Why should we be? Information is a commodity like any other, and the market in it works just the same way as the market in, say coffee or sugar. I'm no more than a broker. Clients come to me and I buy or sell, as the case may be, regardless of who they are. I may not even know who the client is if they're acting through a middle man. Think about it. We're all in the information game. You and me, and Teddy Vickers, and all those other people in the background whom we never see. This is a trade like any other. Because we both happen to be buddies of Teddy Vickers, I know a little more about your circumstances than anyone normally would, and from what I've been told you're going through a rather tough patch. When I mentioned five grand just now it was something I plucked out of the air. It could be six or seven.'

'Or even eight?'

'Or even eight. You can regard the cash factor as flexible. Something to be negotiated. I happen to know that money doesn't ordinarily mean all that much to you, but this is an exceptional situation you find yourself in.'

'I like to sleep at nights,' Kemp said, 'which, poor as I may be, I succeed in doing. I do my best to avoid hassle, and I suspect there could be an awful lot of hassle tucked away in any deal involving a payment for advance notice of where they're going to take up mines to make a safe bathing beach.'

'Why not take a little time to think about it?' Jimson wheedled. 'Reflect. Let's have a further discussion if necessary. Sleep on it. Let's go into all the pros and cons together. I know that when anyone lives as you've lived under a dictatorial regime, you tend to have this feeling that Big Brother's looking over your shoulder. But in this case it's irrational.'

'By picking up a telephone and talking to a friend in the government for five minutes I stand to make about as much as I do in six months' hard work. That worries me. Life isn't like that. I'd call it risk money. Something has to be wrong.'

'The fact is, I've taken you by surprise. This comes out of the blue and naturally you want time to think. What I feel we ought to do is have another meeting. Whatever doubts and objections you may have, I only ask to be given the chance to sort them out. This must be a happy, confident and mutually trusting association. How long are you planning on staying in Malta?'

'I want to take off tomorrow.'

'That's a pity, because it doesn't leave us much time. May I call you in the morning?'

'Make it before nine if you do. After that I'll be out shopping.'

They walked together to the arch and the garden's entrance.

'Right then,' Jimson said. 'I'll give you a ring at eight-thirty.' He reached for Kemp's hand, squeezing it in both his own. Trees trailed a backcloth of black moss against the sky, and a single lamp suspended among them like a luminous fruit shafted its light to disclose small, pointed teeth in the cavern of Jimson's parted lips. Two lovers, motionless on a stone bench, were statuary added to the gardens.

'I'll leave you here,' Jimson said. 'Sleep tight, and we'll talk in the morning.'

He turned away and, moving with agility and extraordinary

21

silence, slipped back into the shadows.

The telephone rang in Kemp's room while he was busy with his breakfast.

'Any fresh ideas on the subject under discussion?' Jimson asked.

'None at all. As I told you I'm not at all happy with certain aspects of what was proposed, and I'd prefer to let the matter rest.'

'I'm sorry to hear that. I was hoping we might have been able to snatch a brief half-hour together and explore the possibility of a fresh approach to the problem.'

'It wouldn't serve any purpose.'

'At least let's keep the lines of communication open. You might think it over and decide to change your mind. Who knows? If you do, and I hope you do, you know where to find me. Just give me a call, say you'd like a further discussion—no more than that—and I'll arrange for someone to be over there on the next plane. One final word. The offer closes in fifteen days.'

'I'll bear that in mind,' Kemp said.

'Okay, then. We'll be in touch.'

Jimson hung up, then immediately dialled Brandsteller in Cairo. 'Eddie, hope I didn't wake you. Thought you'd want to know I saw our friend.'

'How are the prospects?'

'Well, frankly not bright. But I'm far from giving up. You know me, don't you? When I get my teeth in I hang on. I can't guarantee instant results, but I'm going to keep on trying.'

'What was the trouble? Money not enough?'

'It wasn't the money. In the end I practically asked him to name his own figure. Know something? I'd say he was just plain scared.'

'It proves one thing at least,' Brandsteller said. 'The guy has to be straight. What's the next move then?'

'The next move is to find a way of putting on the pressure.

I've talked Vickers into going along with us, and I'm hoping he'll come up with something.'

'Well, keep at it, James, and remember this is the biggest deal we've ever set up together. The reward is proportionate.'

'I'll be in touch as soon as I have anything new to report,' Jimson said.

Kemp went out to do his shopping in Valetta's noisy and precipitous streets. Much as the Libyans were prepared to glut the foreigners in their midst with luxury articles sold in their celebrated hypermarkets, the expatriates continued to yearn for forbidden things: for pork in all its forms and disguises, for shellfish, for literature devoted to violence and sexually explicit themes, for girlie magazines—in short all the abominations outlawed by Muslim puritanism, and any visitor to Malta was expected to smuggle back a little contraband of this kind for distribution among his grateful friends.

Kemp went from grocer to grocer, dutifully burdening himself with the bacon, sausages and salami that would bring so much joy into the lives of a half-dozen acquaintances, and then, with a half-hour to spare before taking a taxi to the airport, settled himself for a coffee in Palace Square.

He was still suffering from a feeling of some bewilderment, even perturbation, following the experience of the previous night. As Kemp saw it, any journalist stationed in a country for a number of years could be expected to know more than most about what was going on behind the scenes. If you wanted to talk to the leader of the underground opposition, in any country, or have a meeting with any guerrillas who happened to be in the mountains, who could always fix it for you? Why, a newspaperman, of course. And newspapermen were accustomed—as he was—to be approached from time to time by persons in search of hidden facts. But there was a protocol to be followed on such occasions. You contrived an introduction to your man. You bought him a good meal in the best restaurant in town—possibly several meals in a row. The assault by hospitality might include a visit to a strip-tease club, and shelling out for what was likely to follow that. A superior prostitute might be brought into the proceedings, or an ex-girlfriend induced to help out. All in good time you put your questions, and waited for the secrets to flow.

This was how it was done, and whatever a relationship developed, it was not damaged by a crude offer of money. There might be journalists who accepted cash payments for what they had to offer, but Kemp had never met one. Jimson, by this approach, had labelled himself an outsider as well as breaking an unwritten law. The best that Valetta had to offer in the way of a night out on the town might have cost £50 a head—say £150, if women came into it—and it was the kind of expenditure that would not have put Kemp on his guard. Instead he had been offered this vast, brutal, compromising sum.

Kemp was beginning now to wonder whether, despite Vickers' character reference, Jimson was what he purported to be, or whether he could be some sort of agent provocateur sent to test Kemp's reliability and the degree of loyalty he owed to a government whose servant he was—even if only on a part-time basis.

Chapter Three

The morning Air Malta flight was packed with expatriates, a majority of them oilmen who had been on shopping trips to the island, many of whom, with outrageous daring, would be carrying not only ritually unclean foods, but whisky transferred to bottles labelled as fruit juice, medicines and non-alcoholic fluids of all kinds.

Most of the passengers faced disembarkation at Tripoli with frayed nerves, conscious of illicit articles stowed away in their baggage, dreading also the ordeal awaiting them at immigration where two separate passport inspections were imposed, and the immaculate and largely silent security men who scrutinized the faces as well as documents of each new arrival seemed endowed with the power of second sight, as well as able, like dogs, to detect the aromas of guilt and fear.

The oilmen downed gins and tonics and whisky sodas as fast as they could be served during their brief flight, both to soften the impact of the coming experience and also in the knowledge that they would taste no more real liquor for months to come. Kemp rationed himself to a single drink, remembering that in any encounter with Arab officials an alcohol-laden breath helped to tip the argument against the traveller. He leafed through a *Newsweek* bought in Malta and certain to be debarred in Tripoli, which he proposed to leave on the plane; when he landed he would be carrying an art magazine with a picture of Renoir's *Baigneuse* on the cover to be used as a decoy when the time came for him to pass through customs.

The plane touched down, taxied to a halt, the doors opened and the passengers poured out of it and began their stampede for the entrance to the airport buildings. Kemp found himself in a hustling queue at the entrance to the Immigration Hall, awaiting the first of the passport inspections. The official snapped open his passport and gestured to him to stand aside. Kemp was surprised and faintly alarmed. He was added to a group of eight persons, several of them visibly drunk, who had come in on the same flight, and a moment later they were marched off to a waiting room. Kemp knew by experience that this was the normal procedure applied to passengers travelling on new passports or who were entering the country for the first time, or who had made the fatal mistake of visiting Israel or Egypt since the granting of their visas; but in all his comings and goings it had never happened to him before. There was something a little unearthly about the atmosphere of the waiting room, as of the airport in general; the hush, the complete absence of notices of any kind, the occasional airborne intoning of announcements in sonorous Arabic, like someone reading from a sacred book. Those who waited here were reduced, vacant of expression, to utter submission, almost to coma. After a while a young man padded up from behind on rubber-soled shoes to touch Kemp on the shoulder. 'John,' he said, 'come with me.' To Arab minor officials they were all Johns, just as in the colonial days all Arabs had been Abdul to the foreigners who ruled.

He took Kemp to the interview room where he was seen by another young man he instantly recognized as a member of the investigatory police drawn principally from Bedouin tribal groups who were supposed to have retained the purity of desert ideals. Kemp had met this young man briefly at the Aïd el Kebir party for students returning from England, where he had squatted, the only European guest among twelve Arabs, to pluck the succulent flesh from a lamb roasted whole. He remembered that this particular ex-tribesman had said, in illustration of the austerity of his childhood scene, that his father had objected to the use of corrugated iron as a building material in village shacks, because it smacked of luxury and decadence.

The young official, like all the members of his branch, had the sincere and hopeful face of a recent religious convert. He gave no sign of recognizing Kemp.

'Sir, you were in Malta for a very short visit. Can you explain to me why you went?'

What a fool I was, Kemp thought. What an unspeakable idiot to draw attention to myself by staying away only twenty-four hours. On the form it had said. 'What is the purpose of the journey for which you are applying for an exit and re-entry visa—business or tourism?' and he had written 'tourism (holiday); because that was what everybody always did, as it meant the difference between getting a visa right away, and sometimes having to wait for weeks on end. The question was whether Vickers' phone call had been monitored, thus putting the investigatory police on his track. It was something he had to take a chance on. 'It was largely a shopping trip,' he said.

'May I ask what you bought?'

'The usual things. Books, gramophone records. Let me see, oh yes, a couple of video cassettes. Tins of food.' Mentioning the last item he turned down the corners of his mouth in a deprecatory fashion as if to say, 'you know how it is. It's the kind of thing we all do'.

The man nodded his sympathy. 'Articles that are not easily obtained here in fact.' He opened Kemp's passport again, handling it with respect, almost with reverence. Something in the movement of his fine hands went with the room's frieze of Arabic lettering, twining and untwining like small delicate serpents. The excessive elegance of the calligraphy slowed Kemp's reading of their message: *Not masters and servants, but equal partners in endeavour.* Kemp felt an inkling of that shadowy false guilt so often experienced by persons under suspicion of an offence they have not committed.

The official was looking at a screen of the kind one sees on the counter of air-terminal check-ins. He pressed some buttons then glanced up.

'You are a journalist. This must involve you in much travel.'

'It used to. Nowadays I'm based here. I assist in the English production of *The Green Standard.*'

'Have you visited Israel?'

'Yes, I have. About five years ago. Before I came here.' Kemp knew it would be all on that screen.

'You went as a journalist?'

'Yes.'

'And you have been to Egypt?'

'Egypt, too. About three months later.'

'You would have used a second passport in that case.'

'I had to, like everyone else. It was the regular thing.'

'Of course. Do you expect to be leaving this country again in the near future?'

'I have no plans to do so,' Kemp said.

The official got up and held out his hand. 'Mr Kemp, I am sorry to have taken up so much of your time. I hope you will enjoy your continued stay with us.'

Kemp had been surprised to see a man called Craddock among those held back for an additional security check, having been under the impression that Craddock had recently left the country on a visit to Egypt. He had avoided his eye in the waiting room, but reaching the customs hall he saw Craddock just ahead, staggering under the baggage he had collected, towards the nearest booth. Craddock was in some vague import-export business, and a man with valuable connections in the black market, both in currency and liquor. Kemp would have preferred to steer clear of him at a time when he believed him to be a little drunk, especially as at the best of times he was prone to argument when stillness and humility were to be recommended. He was making for a vacant booth when a customs officer headed him off and signalled to him to follow Craddock.

By the time Kemp was allowed into the booth one of the customs men was tearing into Craddock's luggage. He pulled a flattish package from the depths of a suitcase, sniffed at it with a wrinkling nose, as if alerted by an odour of decay, before dropping it on to the counter.

'What is this, please?'

'Don't tell me you don't know,' Craddock said. 'Bacon. The cured flesh of the pig, a noble and intelligent animal, whatever you may think.' After four doubles in rapid succession he had thrown caution to the winds. Leaning forward he breathed the fumes of whisky into the man's face.

The customs man shook his head. 'Pig no good.'

'Pig very good.'

Craddock had made an enemy now, and the customs man, fired with new zeal, soon found pork sausages, salami and three tins of ham, which he put aside with gloved hands to await destruction. A packet of Beecham's Powders had ruptured to leak its contents on to the counter.

'What is this, droogs?'

'It's not droogs. It's medicine you b.f. Understand medicine?'

The customs man did not, or at least pretended he did not, and the package was held for analysis. Craddock was given a receipt and dismissed.

Kemp came off lightly. '*Salaam aleikum*,' he said to the man.

The customs officer smiled. '*Wa aleikum es salaam.*'

Kemp took the copy of the art magazine out of his pocket and laid it on his suitcase. The Customs man glanced at Renoir's indecent picture on the cover, shook his head, and confiscated it. Honour satisfied, he marked Kemp's baggage with his chalk and waved him through.

Craddock was waiting for him. 'I thought you were in Cairo,' Kemp said.

'I was. Now I'm back in this bloody awful hole again.' He stared ruefully at Kemp. 'Gave me a hell of a going over. You lose much?'

'Only a magazine with a picture he objected to.'

'Why do these bastards always favour you?'

'They don't. It's only a matter of luck. He took his blood-lust out on you, so I got off lightly.'

'Picked up a haggis for Burns' night in Malta,' said Craddock. 'He actually grabbed that, too.'

A man in a peaked cap had spotted him and waved a sheaf of papers to attract their attention.

'I booked a hire-car,' Craddock said. 'Keep an eye on my gear, I'll go and get it.'

Kemp, who had not ordered a car, was quite happy to share with Craddock. He watched him go storming off into the press of travellers like a swimmer into the breakers of a hostile sea. Kemp stood his ground until a dozen vaguely Pakistani cleaning women in Muslim trousers and upcurled shoes nudged him with their mops into the path of a queue of Rumanians bound for immigration and the departure lounge. The Rumanians were the sharpest dressers of the Eastern bloc. Twelve men in a row wore dinner suits, and most of the women were in long dresses suited to formal occasions, bought at government shops forbidden by religion to make a profit.

Craddock was back. 'Right then. Let's go.'

They piled their luggage into the battered VW. 'Where are you bound for?' Craddock asked.

'Kilometre Seven.'

'Suits me. I'm back in the Compound for the time being.'

They set out into the city's familiar chaos with all the opportunities it offered Westerners for self-complacency and contempt.

'How was Egypt?' Kemp asked.

'Pretty good, but I had quite a bit of explaining to do before they'd let me in again. Mind you, politically things are very dodgy. I was at a reception attended by the President and you can see he's losing touch. Ever run into him while you were over there?'

'Once. He gave a party for the press just after the Yom Kippur war. Funny sort of experience in its way. I often think about it. I noticed he was smiling in my direction and I thought he'd mistaken me for a friend. After a bit he came over and shook me by the hand. "You are Thoth, the messenger," he said. "I understand the message you bring me from the gods." Or words to that effect.'

'Folies de grandeur. He's bonkers. I suspect he always was.'

'Are you still interested in whisky?' Craddock asked.

'Yes,' Kemp said, 'but in original bottles, properly sealed.'

'This is Black Label export. I hope you can trust me by now.'

'How much?'

'Thirty a bottle.'

'Dinars or pounds?'

'Pounds.'

'Where does it come from?'

'I prefer not to tell you that.'

'Forget it, then. I'm not in the market.'

'All right, it's one of the Leader's personal pilots.'

'You know him?'

'Yes I do. A very good man. One of us.' By this he meant that the pilot was white.

'How soon could I have delivery?'

'He's out of the country now. Probably next week. Ten days at most.'

'I'm interested,' Kemp said. 'Let me know when you have a firm date.'

'Will do,' Craddock said. He let out a sudden squawk of delight to draw Kemp's attention to the balconies of a new block of flats they were passing crowded with the animals—including one baby camel—of the peasants who occupied them. Another joyful outcry followed at the spectacle of a car which had mounted another as if in an act of copulation; thus joined, the cars had embedded themselves in the wall of a house.

They were back to the black market again. 'Giving a party, are you?' Craddock asked.

'In the near future. It's my turn.'

'If you find thirty a bottle a lot to pay, you could start off with Black Label and top up with flash.'

'I couldn't,' Kemp said.

'Genuine home-distilled stuff, I mean, costing you half the price. Save a lot of money.'

'Wouldn't dream of it,' Kemp told him.

'Why not?'

'Because I have to keep out of trouble, and I'm prepared to pay just to do that. I work for these people and so far I get on well with them. I wouldn't want to risk losing my villa.'

'You know best,' Craddock said.

They parked the car as near as they could get to the villa, and dodged the holes and the mounds of builder's rubble to cover the final fifty yards on foot. A year before, bulldozers had arrived to open up a series of trenches like those of the First World War. The intention had been to lay drains but it turned out that the drains were already there; although the bulldozers were withdrawn the trenches remained. These were slowly filling with abandoned mechanisms and the occasional dead animal. This had been a select resort area where Italian plutocrats had come to disport themselves in bygone summers. The Arabs pointed almost with disbelief to the caverns in some gardens where rabbits had been reared in total darkness, to provide the courtesans who accompanied them with their almost transparent flesh, supposed to nourish ardour without increasing weight.

Nowadays most of the villas were tenanted by the new sober-minded Arab aristocracy, who had added a little icing sugar decoration, and stained glass where they could. Kemp's villa, among the broken brick and rampant jasmine, remained untouched. Craddock, seeing it for the first time, shook his head in wonder.

'Seven or eight rooms would there be?' he asked.

'Seven, plus a fair-sized entrance hall.'

'Couple of bathrooms?'

'Three.'

'Best villa in Kilometre Seven, is it?'

'One of the best.'

'How do you do it?'

'I suppose they value my services at *The Green Standard*. They find me useful in one way or another.'

'I've often wondered what makes you stay here? They give you this villa, a better car than most of us can afford to drive, and I'm sure the money's good. But is that all that matters?'

A jealous man, Kemp thought. He smiled broadly. 'I'll let you into a secret. I happen to believe that, whether you like it or not, this is a country with a future. Therefore it offers opportunities.'

'So that's it,' Craddock said. 'I've often wondered.'

Kemp rang the bell on the gate and Mike appeared instantly to open it, the dog at his side. Mike Jolly was a kindly, unambitious man, who had once been temporary Assistant Third Secretary at the Embassy. Now he had turned himself into a professional villa-sitter, employed to keep out squatters by those who went on leave, or were absent from home for more than a single night; and his services were in constant demand. The dog, a deerhound of noble imperturbability, reached forward to sniff at the air about six inches from Kemp's crutch. It was its way of making a racial decision, and it had been trained to show suspicion and, if necessary, hostility to persons of non-Caucasian origin. Kemp passed the test, and the dog backed away to allow him through.

'Nice trip?'

'Very. Malta's a good spot out of season. Recommend it.'

They went up onto the roof, a sundown ritual in these parts. One of the few local features wholeheartedly admired by the expatriates were the desert sunsets, which in this case, although the desert was well out of sight behind unfinished high-rise blocks, still stained their skin with a vivacious glow.

Mike brewed a reasonable beer from supplies of Bio-Malt he bought up whenever this product appeared on the market. This they sipped while they exchanged gossip.

'Didn't expect you back so soon,' Mike said. 'What happened?'

'I managed to clear up what I had to do in a few hours. No point in hanging on. I had things to get back to. Anything much been going on?'

'Not a great deal. You heard Intair bent a derrick?'

'Scott told me about it before I left.'

'The Phantom Bottom-Biter bit again yesterday. Girl was bending over to load up her car in the hypermarket park, and he got her. Made his getaway in a BMW.'

'How did you hear about it?'

'It was in the Arab papers. He's a European disguised as an Arab, they said.'

'And they probably believe it.'

'The police are going to crack down on the booze barons,' Mike said.

Kemp's nerves gave a start. 'Who told you that?'

'My contact on the inside. This is for sure. The feeling among the indigenous is that enough is enough.'

'It sounds like bad news to me.'

'Why? You're not into booze, are you?

'No, but I keep it in the house, and I serve it to friends. This could fall back on all of us.'

'We've asked for it,' Mike said. 'We're turning into a collection of alcoholics. I was at the Clinic for a check-up, and one of the medics told me that one expat in six has a drink problem. That's something that frightens me, Ron.'

'It's the poison most people are obliged to drink,' Kemp said.

'I hope you're right. What worries me is whether we're losing our grip as a people.'

They sipped their mild, innocent beer, watching the sea feathered by a small evening breeze beyond the filigree of wreckage strewn along the shore. A gull overhead mewed its loneliness, and a procession of Americans jogged into their field of vision and out again. They were in an area set aside by the authorities for the purpose after a jogger had been arrested under the belief that any running man must be a criminal escaping from justice.

'Very warm for the time of the year, isn't it? Mike said. 'Any news of the promised beach?'

'Not a word.'

'I suppose we have to go on hoping,' Mike said.

'Only thing we can do.'

'I knew there was something I had to tell you. Wendy got out of prison.'

'My God, I'd forgotten all about her. How is she?'

'A bit shattered, as is to be expected, but not too bad on the whole. The main thing is, she's changed.'

'In what way?'

'She used to be fresh and sweet when she first arrived, and then she changed, and we all know why. Now she's changed back. In a way you could say the experience seems to have done her good. Apart from that I think we all ought to make an effort and rally round.'

'Where is she at the moment?' Kemp asked.

'She's staying in the Watsons' house in the Compound while they're away.'

'I'll make a point of popping over there to see her.'

'Be nice if you would. She'd really appreciate that. She needs to have her friends around at a time like this.'

Chapter Four

By seven-thirty Kemp was out distributing what he had brought back for people whose life, wherever and however they might live, was incomplete without long-back bacon, kipper fillets, Cooper's marmalade, and Alka-Seltzer. There were also special requests to be delivered in the way of nostalgic records of song-hits of the thirties, a video tape of the Royal Wedding, Korean red ginseng, and a preparation called 'Stop ... Stop', bought from a Maltese agent of a lady who ran a chain of sex shops in the U.K.

His appointment with the Editor of *The Green Standard* was for midday, and he made a short detour on his way there in the new Peugeot supplied by the General Board of Tourism and Fairs to visit Wendy Winters. Wendy, a notable alcoholic who had succumbed to the pressures exerted on a single girl by the expatriate life, had spent a month in the woman's prison for drunken and disorderly conduct and for assaulting a police officer who had finally felt obliged to arrest her. Kemp found her in the Watsons' bungalow in the act of attending to the requirements of the insect-eating plants the Watsons, who were home on leave, had collected as an antidote to the extreme monotony of their surroundings.

'And you don't mind talking about it,' Kemp asked her.

'Not in the slightest. It makes me feel better. In a way I'm even grateful all this happened. I realize now what I was heading for.'

Mike was right. She was quite different. There had always been a hinted asceticism in the wasted beauty of her features, and now this had taken command. It was a face suited to penance.

She dropped the last fly into the last vegetable throat, and then switched on the kettle to make tea.

'I underwent a personality change,' she explained. 'I was full of anger. Angry with everything and everyone. It's terrible not to be able to stop being angry.'

'That's the effect flash seems to have in a lot of cases. Some people can take it and others can't. Question of the central nervous system.'

'The place they put me in was like a ghastly sort of hospital. Most of the girls were in for shoplifting. You can't imagine what hypermarkets have done to them.'

'Good thing they don't cut hands off any more.'

Small lines showed hopefully at the corners of her mouth but the smile never broke through. She seemed to have worn out her capacity for mirth. 'Half the female population would be going round with only one hand if they did that,' she said. 'They had women psychologists to discuss your problems with you, but they really couldn't get to grips with the idea of a rich female drunkard. The only thing that came any lower for them was an adulteress. Funny mixture, aren't they? It's more acceptable to walk out of a shop with half a dozen dresses stuffed down your pants, or even to stick a knife in someone, than sleep around. In other ways they're a bit more civilized than us. I used to be a prison visitor at Holloway once upon a time.'

'So what's it to be now, Wendy? Will you be staying on?'

'Of course I will. I've got my job back, and I'm starting again next week. Everybody's been absolutely wonderful. I'm back with Bill.'

'I didn't even know there'd been any problem there.'

'Well, there had. And he's been wonderful to have done what he's done. After all I put him through, he was there to meet me when I came out.'

'It's no more than I would have expected.'

'Trouble is people like me let other people down all the time. We don't mean it. It's a disease, a real disease.'

'Bill understands that. He's big enough to understand. Where is he now?'

'Still down on the rig at Sidi Hocine. But they've agreed to shift him back to town headquarters so that we can be together. He's coming up next week.'

'I hope I'll see him. Hope to see you both. We must get together. Listen, I'm giving a party. Would you and Bill come along?'

'It's sweet of you, Ron, and I'd like to very much, and I know Bill would, too. But can I take a rain-check on that one?'

'Come if you can. Make an effort, won't you? It's been a long time.'

'Let's leave it this way, if we're in a party-going mood we will. If we don't show I know you'll understand.'

'Of course I will.'

He kissed the smooth concavity of her cheek lightly. 'Lovely to see you looking so well,' he said. 'And congratulations about Bill. It's been marvellous news.'

'A story with a happy ending for once,' she said.

Kemp arrived at the office of *The Green Standard* at a moment when a small flock of fat-tailed sheep left by a visitor in the entrance hall had broken free from the custody of the boy left to guard them, causing the electric-eye operated lift-doors to open and close repeatedly as he went in to chase.

He bypassed the sheep and went up to see the editor, Mr Salim. The movement of every moveable object in the editor's office was under electric control, and a state of potential flux had been extended to the dimension of the room itself, variable by partitions which advanced or receded, provided there were no power cuts or jammed circuits when Mr Salim twisted a dial. 'We are surrounded by so many sophisticated things,' Salim was accustomed to say, with a kind of uneasy pride. Sophisticated was a word rarely out of people's mouths. On the occasion of Kemp's first visit to Mr Salim they had stood together at the window to watch a military parade pass beneath, and the leading tank, far too sophisticated for its driver, had left the line to spin in a circle, then carry on as before, garlanded with a ceremonial arch.

The two men discussed the last issue of *The Green Standard*, an English-language sheet printed on expensive paper, smelling faintly of rose-petals. Two years before, at the beginning of their association, Kemp had limited his involvement to a few gently-phrased criticisms of its aggrieved and belligerent style. Since then he had expanded and remodelled the paper, pruned out all the stale political jargon, and added a women's page, achieving, to the Arabs' delight, a six-fold increase in circulation. Salim, a good friend, remained editor in name only, and recently overtures had been made to Kemp as to the possibility of his taking all foreign-language publications under his wing.

Their last meeting, some days previously, had followed a curious circumstance when Kemp, arriving without an appointment, had practically collided with a tall, severe-faced, white-bearded Arab, wearing a high turban and black gown, coming out of Salim's office. The lift was out of order and when the man asked Kemp to be directed to the stairs Kemp picked up his unmistakable Egyptian accent and use of words.

There was something furtive in Salim's expression when Kemp mentioned the incident. 'An old-fashioned religious gentleman,' Kemp said. 'You don't see too many of his kind about these days. Didn't even know there were any Egyptians in the country.'

Salim was on the defensive. His face belonged to the past of the craftsmen who had been his forbears, and Kemp might have been a customer in the souk drawing attention to some small imperfection in an article offered for sale.

'This man was a doctor in theology,' he said. 'His visit here is welcome. We have no quarrel with the people of Egypt. It is only their leaders who have betrayed them who are our enemies.'

What's going on here? Kemp asked himself. Why the worried look?

While talking Kemp had skimmed through most of the paper's articles. 'I'll take this away, go over it at home, and come back to you if anything occurs to me.'

'That would be very kind of you.'

'The main thing is to promote better understanding,' Kemp said. 'To reduce the feeling of isolation experienced by so many British and Americans who expect to spend some of their best years working in your country. And as far as possible to ease certain restrictions.'

'That is important. We want to do all we can.'

'In that context, you remember the last story I put on the wire to London about the five-year plan for tourism? Is there any more news of the beach?'

'It has been agreed. The only question now is where it is to be sited. We are open to suggestions.'

'I haven't really any ideas on the subject. It wants to be a good safe beach with plenty of sand, free from dangerous currents and underwater rocks, and as near the centre of town as possible.'

'If we can find such a site I would like you to inspect it and pass your opinions. It would be of help to us.'

'I should be glad to do that.'

Their main business was now at an end, and Salim turned to polite enquiries about Kemp's new villa, found for him despite huge difficulties in the matter of accommodation, largely through the Board's efforts.

'It's excellent in every way,' Kemp assured him. 'Spacious, airy, beautiful view over the sea.'

The moment seemed right to give notice of the forthcoming party, and to sound out Salim's views on the subject.

'I'd like to give a little house-warming party in the near future. Can you see any difficulties arising?'

'Why should they arise?'

'All my neighbours are highly respectable, rather retiring people. They live very quietly. I wouldn't like to offend them.'

'In what way could your party offend them?'

'We're sometimes inclined to be a little noisy. When my fellow expatriates get together they tend to let their hair down.'

'Your neighbours will make allowances,' Salim said. 'You are guests in this country.'

'Thank you.'

'I will check who your neighbours are. Perhaps I could even telephone them to explain. Will many friends be attending your party?'

'Quite a few. Probably more than I bargain for.'

'Women as well as men?'

'It's our custom.'

'Of course it is. The parties we hold separately for the two sexes are less interesting. In some ways we are still far behind the times.'

'It's all a question of tradition.'

'Do Western ladies also drink whisky?'

'I'm afraid they do. When they can get it.'

'We are bound to become more broadminded, but progress is still slow. A scene was shown here on the television of a man and woman kissing and some people broke their sets. There is a man in this building who operates a sophisticated computer, who is accustomed to order his wife and daughters to veil themselves when a male announcer appears on the screen. There will be dancing at your party, of course?'

'It's unavoidable. Hence the noise. However, be sure of this, I will keep it as quiet as I can.'

'I know you will, Mr Kemp. I am sure that there will be no problem.'

Kemp detected something wistful in Salim's manner. Probably jump at an invitation, he thought. 'Why don't you come?' he said. 'Be a bit of an experience. You might quite enjoy it.'

'Well, perhaps I will. Thank you. Perhaps I will.'

'It's provisionally fixed for the twenty-fifth. I hope you can make it. Starts at seven. Be glad to see you.'

'Thank you. I will try to be there.'

Chapter Five

The meeting with Salim over, Kemp found himself at a loose end. He drove over to the telegraph office to put a routine story on the wire, called on several contacts in the souk to take coffee with them, then drove back to the villa to do what he could with the evening.

He put the finishing touches to a letter to his wife Claire, explaining why he had come to a decision to spend at least two more years in Libya. '*Of course it's hideously uncomfortable and you won't find an expat with a good word to say for it. It's all perverse enthusiasms, mess and muddle, but this is where the action is—and you know me. Not a day without some new challenge. Any other Arab country is a backwater by comparison.*' And that, he decided, laying down the letter, was no exaggeration.

This was a time when Kemp was beginning to feel acutely deprived of feminine company. For every five western males in Tripoli, there was only one female. The problem was exaggerated by the fact that half the women were married, under guard of husbands who watched over them like Turks. A number of oil companies imported unmarried female staff, but it was their policy to favour mature applicants, less prone, according to their experience, than younger women to succumb to the temptations and the wilder forms of escapism offered by the environment. These, whatever their age, even appearance, were in huge demand. Only recently Kemp had paid vigorous and successful court to a lady accountant in her fifties, who had dropped him after a few felicitous weeks for a younger man.

The ironic part was that until now the great shortage of accommodation had compelled Kemp to share a house with a chemical analyst with strait-laced views who objected to women being brought in, and the ladies he had been most successful with, from decorous backgrounds and approaching middle years, insisted on a sedate and orderly setting for their encounters, which ruled out the back of a car concealed in a corner of a scrap-iron dump. The alternatives were few. Every hotel displayed a notice, 'No Visitors Admitted to Rooms', a prohibition he had only once evaded by a gift of expensive perfume to the receptionist in a small Spanish-owned hotel.

Now at last he had his own villa, one of the best in town and enough rooms in it to house a harem, but it was empty. His footfalls trailed echoes through the thinly furnished rooms, and even the small pockets of disorder he cultivated in the absence of the Filipino girl who worked for him, continued their stubborn denial that the place was really lived in. Two large pictures in ornate frames had survived from the Italian days when the villa had belonged to a general; portraits of grandees in evening dress whose eyes seemed determined to avoid his. An aseptic something in the air neutralized any of the odours of occupation. When Mike Jolly had departed both the strong reek of his local cigarettes and of his dog went with him. The neighbouring villas were occupied by rich Arabs, but Kemp had never seen a face at any of their windows. Salim had once said to him, 'Mr Kemp, the impression that I have of you is that you are a lonely man. Yes, a lonely man.' On the whole, Salim had been mistaken, but at this moment Kemp would have agreed with him that this was so.

At 7.30 Kemp switched on the television when the principal channel contributed two hours to the English-speaking community. The current offering was *Your Life in Their Hands*, and Kemp found himself watching an operation for cancer of the stomach—the most popular episode in the most popular series ever shown, acclaimed so enthusiastically by viewers of both races and religions, that this was its third repeat. A Muslim of religious standing had even been called in to give a ruling that whereas the human body in prime and vigorous condition ought not to be seen by members of the opposite sex, any pathological state freed it from the ban.

Kemp watched the excision of a fearful tumour while toying with the curry the Filipino girl had left for him, which had become less appetizing. There was something in the unveiling of this secret horror, in the masked inhumanity of the surgeons at their work, that increased his feeling of isolation. After a few minutes he switched off. He tossed the remnant of the curry into the waste bin, washed up, and decided to free himself from the stagnant atmosphere of the place for an hour or two.

The Tourist Board had built a luxury hotel, the Omar El Muktar at Kilometre Nine, and he drove to it along the coast road, now deserted except for handsome desert dogs that slept in the car-cemeteries of that area by day, and came out to hunt in packs after dark. The hotel, outlined in lights like a cavern of sparkling jewels opened to the night, catered in the main to delegations from the Eastern bloc, but unattached Western oilmen, driven to desperation by the longing for feminine proximity, went there in the unrealistic hope of sexual adventure. A rumour was current that Eastern bloc female delegates were broadminded and easy to approach. They were also said to be kept very short of money, with the result that some were prepared to make their persons available, if tactfully appealed to, for as little as 25 dinars—the equivalent of £28.

There was nothing stand-offish about the delegates—as Kemp took them to be—circulating in the lounge, and at a receptive glance from a golden-haired, intelligent-looking young woman, he drew up a chair at her table and sat down. She told him instantly, in perfect English, that she was a lecturer in Moldavian painted churches. Kemp could see from the many strings of pearls she wore that she had been on a shopping spree, and the hint of a materialist outlook encouraged him. 'Do you find they pay you enough?' he began hopefully, but it was a question she clearly did not understand.

He excused himself and went to drink a nauseous concoction of fruit juices at the bar. Why had the Arabs become like this? he asked himself. Why the puritanism? He remembered that even at the beginning of his stay in the country things had been different. Even then, in the years before they had begun the dismantling of the souk, there were snug little retreats in its alleyways where a decent, civilized and even romantic encounter could be organized between solitary strangers and a well-conducted local girl.

A thing of the past, alas. He paid for his drink, mooched disconsolately through the public rooms for a few minutes and then, quite suddenly, was taken ill.

He reached a terrace lined with scented plants in tubs, which he sluiced with bitter vomit. After that he managed to grope his way to his car, haul himself into the driving seat, and drive home. He went in a drunkard's rush to the telephone to call a Swiss company doctor called Blanchard, the only one of his profession bold enough to come out at night. 'I think I'm dying,' he told him.

Blanchard was at the door within fifteen minutes, and Kemp explained his symptoms between groans and spasms of retching. 'I have a kind of blurred, double vision. You appear to be moving sideways. All sensation in my fingers has gone. I keep grinding my teeth.'

'You've been poisoned,' Blanchard said. 'Where did you go tonight?'

'The Omar el Muktar.'

'What did you drink?'

'A Jamaica.'

'Nothing else?'

'No.'

'Have you ever quarrelled with a waiter there? Made complaints? Sent food back?'

'Never.'

Kemp pressed his hand over his stomach where something squirmed like a trapped animal under the flesh.

'What did you have for your last meal?' Blanchard asked.

'Curry.'

'From a tin?'

'Fresh. The girl who looks after the place cooked it for me.'

'Had any trouble with her? Given her any cause for

offence?'

'Not that I know of.'

'I must warn you that it's very common here for native people to use poisons when love affairs go wrong.'

'There's never been anything between us, and in any case she's a Filipino, not a local.'

'Whatever happened, I know the symptoms, and they are those of a native poison called ts'hur. I'm going to get you to hospital as fast as I can. We can't wait for an ambulance. I'll take you in my car.'

Blanchard rang the hospital to arrange for a bed then gave Kemp an injection. 'This will calm you down,' he said. 'They may use a stomach pump, which isn't pleasant. If they decide on a body respirator, it will be in readiness for use. The thing is they have everything that's necessary.'

There was a splash of vomit on the edge of the bowl Kemp had been using, and Blanchard used a spatula to remove a trace of this, which he sealed in an envelope and put away in his case.

Blanchard drove Kemp to the 14th May Clinic normally used by oilmen and their dependants, where he had arranged for Kemp's admission. Kemp was carried on a stretcher into the casualty department where, after a short discussion with two doctors on duty, Blanchard left him.

One of the doctors then explained to Kemp, so sedated by this time that he could hardly grasp what was being said, that a mistake had been made and he was to be taken to the Oasis Hospital.

He was given a second injection, floated away into semi-consciousness, felt nothing of the ambulance ride, and took in little of the surroundings when he arrived beyond an impression of banked flowers, soft music and reassuring smiles. He drifted, pillowed on air, from scene to scene, peered at by masked faces, and soothed by the touch of soft hands. Electrodes were attached to parts of his body, a tube passed into his rectum and another down his throat into the stomach but he felt neither apprehension nor discomfort. Finally sleep carried him away, and he awoke next morning as if from a weird dream, in what he first took to be a room in a luxury hotel.

All the symptoms of the night before had left him. He felt weak, but relaxed, poised as it were, on the brink of euphoric visions promoted by the opiates in his blood. The Oasis Hospital was the newest and finest of its kind in the country. Oil resources had paid for the most advanced equipment and had hired the services of some of the best medical brains to be discovered from a dozen countries. Kemp lay smiling at the ceiling. A manufactured and adjustable breeze dusted spices over him and stirred the bed coverlet. Starched nurses bustled in and out trailing faint arpeggios of string music, and from time to time a doctor with a central European accent would appear at his bedside to question him with extreme earnestness on his sensations. Later he enjoyed the amenities of a five-star hotel, including newspapers only a day late from England, choice of fat-free food from an extensive à la carte menu, and viewing on the latest Sony television, the first programme being a further episode of *Your Life in Their Hands*, showing an operation to replace the knee joints.

Dr Abd Er Rahman, a senior consultant and a jolly, bumbling man, visited him and stuck a sprig of jasmine in the vase by his bedside. It was his second morning in hospital and Kemp, refreshed and optimistic, put aside the *Financial Times* delivered with his breakfast.

'Any verdict yet as to what happened to me?' Kemp asked. 'I hear I may have been poisoned.'

Abd Er Rahman's almost continuous laughter broke off into a cough.

'Who told you that?'

'Dr Blanchard.'

'What does Dr Blanchard mean by poisoned? One can say that most severe infections of the digestive tract are caused by poisoning.'

Something like anxiety had suddenly thinned and sharpened the fleshy companionable face. He's taken me seriously, Kemp thought. But why the panic? 'I imagine that's what he meant,' he said.

'You suffered a mild attack of Type B botulism,' Abd Er Raham said. 'In so far as any such attack can be called mild. This responded to emergency treatment and the usual antidotes. Progress has been satisfactory but it will be necessary to keep you here under observation for a few days to check that no degenerative changes have occurred to liver or kidneys.' His manner was formal to the point of sternness. Something had come between them.

The visit of Dr Ahmed, the Medical Director, took place that evening after the arrival of the night staff, when the routines of the day were at an end, and a hush had fallen on the wards. Abd Er Rahman, a Tunisian of the old school, saturated with the civilized tolerances of that relaxed country had seemed to Kemp to lack strong beliefs. By contrast Dr Ahmed appeared tense and watchful, although his expression was curiously inert, subdued perhaps by long practised control. It was a visit that surprised Kemp, who knew enough about large hospitals to realize that medical directors were not in the habit of visiting patients, other than very rich men or important politicians.

'Mr Kemp, I must tell you that I am distressed about a report that you believe yourself to have been deliberately poisoned.'

'I don't believe anything of the kind, doctor.'

'But surely this is what you told Dr Abd Er Rahman.'

'What I told Dr Abd Er Rahman was that it had been suggested to me I might have been poisoned. I don't remember the actual words used. I made a bit of a joke of it.'

'This is something I cannot laugh at,' Dr Ahmed said. 'Poisoning is offensive to the religious philosophy of the people of my country.'

'And to any other country, I would imagine.'

'Your attack was caused by the exotoxin produced by clostridium botulism; underprocessed foods, in particular meat and fish are usually to blame.'

Kemp preferred to tell the man whatever he wanted to hear, and get rid of him. 'That's the answer, quite obviously,' he said. 'I'd hardly been back in this country a day when this happened. I had to over-night in Malta, and it's possible I picked up something there.'

'What did you eat?'

'Stew with a fancy name. I thought it had a metallic taste.'

'That indeed is the answer. Here we have the explanation.'

In the pause that followed, lasting perhaps three seconds, Kemp had the sensation that they were both playing parts, and there had been a lightning shift in the stage-scenery and mood of the occasion. A fine restructuring of the lines of Dr Ahmed's face had provided him with a made-to-order expression that was conciliatory and confiding.

'Tell me, Mr Kemp, how do you like our hospital?'

'I'm more than impressed, doctor. Much as I'm frightened to think what all this is going to cost.'

'It will cost very little indeed. Far less than a private bed in a hospital in your own country. We consider the Oasis to be the best hospital in Africa.'

'I can believe that's true.'

'At all events you enjoy being with us?'

'The outside world is going to seem a hard place when the time comes to go. And when, by the way, is that likely to be?'

'If your liver continues to behave, you will be ready to get back to work in four or five days.'

'Good. This happens to have hit me in the middle of a busy period.'

'I understand that, because I am familiar with your work as a newspaper correspondent, and I know of the help you have given my friend Mustaffa Salim. May I make a suggestion? If you feel strong enough say tomorrow, or the next day, to work from your bed, I can arrange for a secretary to come in, and should there be any persons you require to interview they may also come here.'

'That's very kind. I may take you up.'

There was another slight re-alignment in the geography of the doctor's features. 'Mr Kemp, may I ask you a personal question? What brought you to this country? The financial inducement?'

'No, doctor, it was not. The financial prospects seemed

attractive, but more than that I enjoy dynamic situations. I believed this country had a long way to go, and I hoped to be able to contribute a little to its future, and therefore to my own.'

'That is understandable. Do you approve of what we're doing? Of the revolutionary changes in our society?'

'As long as they work, I do. The trouble with revolutions is they so often don't.'

'Only because they are sabotaged by the enemies they create. We feel that many members of the foreign community are opposed to us. Some, even, are our enemies.'

'That's putting it far too strongly. I doubt if too many of the multi-nationals are on your side, but most expatriates like myself have no strong political feelings. We're inclined to say, get on with your revolution so long as you leave us in peace. On the whole people worry a lot more about their own comfort than what you happen to be doing in Chad. They object to the restrictions imposed by Islamic countries. They'd like to be able to have a drink when they feel like it. A partnership of equals, as you put it, is all very commendable, but in practice it works out that a family can't even hire a baby-sitter when they feel like a night out.'

'We are very egalitarian. The distribution of wealth is the most equable of any African country. Where else in Africa will you not see a beggar on the streets?'

'Probably nowhere. I agree with you.'

'You feel no sympathy with our struggle?'

'Sympathies are something I'm professionally opposed to. I report on what happens, without comment. You're a surgeon, aren't you?'

'I am.'

'Do you feel sympathy and involvement when you're doing your work? Of course you don't. You're detached. You have to be or the work suffers. And so am I.'

'That is true. It comes out in your writing. You seem to have no personal involvement, and no viewpoint. Therefore your readers believe what you tell them.'

'Which is what good journalism is all about. It's something

that gives me a good deal of satisfaction.'

'You have a strong credibility. Yes, that is true.'

'I've worked hard for it,' Kemp said. 'Something I've built up over the years, just as a businessman builds up the goodwill of his business.'

He felt quite certain now that this was far more than a courtesy visit, and that Dr Ahmed wanted something of him, which the doctor himself realized might be difficult to extract. But in what way could he serve the interests of the Medical Director of a hospital? It was a mystery that the doctor instantly cleared up. 'I must explain to you,' he said, 'that in addition to my medical responsibilities I'm involved with our Directorate of Information.'

'They produce some impressive handouts,' Kemp said. 'The cost must be enormous.'

'That is a very small part of the operation.'

'I imagine so.'

'The Directorate of Information is engaged in many other tasks. There is one aspect of its work in which your co-operation would be of great value.'

'Was that why you came to see me?' Kemp asked.

'Yes.'

Kemp experienced a moment of cautious elation. The Ministry of Tourism and Fairs was small beer, while The Directorate of Information was prestigious and powerful.

'Are you suggesting the possibility of employment with the Directorate, doctor?'

'Official employment would not suit our purpose,' Ahmed said. 'The relationship would be a confidential one. You would retain your connection with Tourism and Fairs and continue to work in your normal way.'

'I see,' Kemp said. The pendulum of his spirits swung back in the other direction. 'Perhaps you should tell me what you mean by co-operation?'

'I am, as you say, putting out feelers. At this stage I would prefer not to be specific. My hope is to uncover a favourable attitude.'

'You don't give me anything to go on. What can I say?'

'An emergency has arisen in which your help would be of the greatest possible assistance to us.'

'But in what way, Doctor? Why the shadow boxing?'

'Would it make things clearer if I tell you that we should require you to renounce your neutrality?'

'A little, but not much. But it's a very tall order, and something that would take a lot of thinking about.'

'The reward would be substantial.'

'Are you proposing to buy me?'

The doctor's guarded but sympathetic smile seemed intended to steer them, like a guide dog, over a tricky terrain.

'You don't say anything, doctor, from which I can only conclude you agree. I'm not sure that I'd like to think of myself as a mercenary.'

'A mercenary is no use to us, Mr Kemp. We ask for commitment.'

'Which is something I can't offer, because it's something I don't possess.'

'Could you acquire it?'

'Certainly not to order.'

It was a disappointing conversation. For a moment Kemp had felt himself on the verge of some significant development in his career. Now he had begun to suspect that there was nothing behind this dubious approach more than a proposition by which he would be induced to tamper with and disarm dangerous news in the way that a bullfighter will secretly shave the horns of a difficult bull. An unpleasant thought occurred to him. Was it possible that the many favours he had received had been designed to soften him up in preparation for this overture? He decided not. Preferential treatment had been going on over too long a period of time, and he had always done anything he could in return. Nothing could make him believe that people like Salim had had an axe to grind.

'To go back to your demand for commitment,' Kemp said, 'it wouldn't be possible while I remain a journalist, because the two things don't go together. I might be able to acquire commitment, as you put it, but in a different occupational context. Which, in any case, is something you don't want. So all in all, doctor, I'm obliged to reject your nebulous appeal, while thanking you for your offer.'

Dr Ahmed got up instantly, and held out his hand. Whatever disappointment he might have felt, nothing of this showed.

Next day brought a change of nurses. The serious, bespectacled young lady from Singapore originally in attendance was replaced by one from Beirut, the possessor of a surprising combination of hair that fell a little short of black, olive skin, and blue eyes. She spoke with a slight American accent, a lively, communicative girl, who soon supplied the clues to the surprises in her colouration. 'My mother is Lebanese,' she said, 'and my father was American working in the Embassy. We moved to Washington and Dad was killed in a car crash. After that Mother and I went home. As soon as I was through high school I took up nursing.'

Things were looking up, Kemp thought. Nurses in Tripoli enjoyed extraordinary status, and were reserved for top management in the oil business.

'We have something in common,' he told her. 'I was in Beirut for years covering the troubles for an English newspaper. I rented a house in Midday Street. The Nufs en Nehar.'

She shook her head in wonderment.

'Do you know it, then?' Kemp asked.

'We lived there before we went to America. It was a beautiful part of Beirut.'

'It was Venice without the canals,' Kemp said. 'All those houses with arched doorways and pointed windows.'

'They smashed the whole district to pieces,' she told him. 'There's nothing left. Remember the tree on the Nufs en Nehar? Even the tree's gone.'

'The Christians, so-called, I suppose?'

The blue eyes contained the gentlest approach. 'We were a

Christian family, but there were Palestinians living all round. People hardly noticed the difference until the troubles started. When they blew the Palestinians' houses up, they blew ours up too, and we went into the camp. We stayed there for a year.'

Kemp was overwhelmed by the coincidence, by their shared memory of an ancient olive tree growing in the middle of a busy road, scarred by so many cars that had collided with it.

'I used to be told it was the luck of the district,' he said. 'No one could cut it down because it belonged to so many families.'

'Beirut was a wonderful place in those days,' she said.

'What brought you here?' he asked.

'What brings anybody here?'

'The money?'

'It was impossible to refuse. I was offered seven times what I was earning in Beirut. We're poor people now. I send back three quarters of my salary and it keeps the whole family going.'

'Any plans to go home?'

'I don't even think about it. I changed nationality, and that means you're here to stay.'

'Not much of a life for you, surely, outside your work? Do you even go out?'

'If you're a woman you soon accept that you don't, except in a group. Once in a while we make up a party among the staff, and go to the Shati or the Chicken on Wheels. It's not much fun because when you have to live in you need a change of faces as well as a change of scene.'

'That is something we all need, Kemp said. 'A change of faces.'

Their conversation was cut short by the arrival of Craddock, fighting for breath after a walk up twelve flights of stairs, through a power cut and the consequent non-functioning of the lifts.

He swivelled slowly to catalogue the room's contents, then moved to the window for the view of the five date palms out of twenty-five that had survived their uprooting from the rich humus of the Oasis of Mizda, and replanting here in subsoil containing more plastic rubbish than earth. At that moment the sun had rounded a corner of the building and the slats of the blind adjusted themselves with a faint click to cut off the direct light. He turned back to Kemp, his face twitching like the flank of a horse troubled by flies. 'How much is all this setting you back?' he asked.

'About a tenner a day.'

'Rubbish.'

'It's true.'

'Wonderful how they do it, isn't it? All this and a beauty queen thrown in to hold your hand. Don't tell me that was a nurse. This is where they send people like the top Palestinian ragheads. What are you doing in here anyway?'

'The diagnosis is Type B botulism.'

'Botulism, eh. I thought that was serious?'

'They've got it under control. Blanchard took me to the Clinic but they didn't have a bed.'

'Too many oilmen suffering from alcoholism and cirrhosis of the liver,' Craddock said.

He picked a magnificent Sicilian grape from the bunch on Kemp's bedside table, rubbing with a kind of angry disbelief at the dove-grey patina of its bloom before thrusting it into his mouth. 'Somebody I know wants to get shot of dinars,' he said. 'They're going at two to the pound for a limited period only.'

'Not interested,' Kemp said.

'The booze is here. We can pick it up when you like.'

'Where is it?'

'The Scotsman is looking after it. How many bottles do you want him to keep for you.'

'Ten,' Kemp said. 'On one condition.'

'What's that?'

'That I can pick a bottle at random, open it and test it.'

'I'll tell him,' Craddock said. 'Whether he'll wear it is another matter. He won't deliver. You'll have to arrange collection yourself.'

'Anything else new on the business front?' Kemp asked.

'Not to interest you. I picked up an order for a thousand garments last week.' Craddock had mentioned that he was an agent for a Manchester firm specializing in the manufacture of garishly patterned and shapeless women's dresses for the Middle Eastern trade. 'I turn my hand to anything,' he explained. 'Have them in all the markets by Ramadhan.'

He had picked up the chart at the bottom of Kemp's bed, and was studying it. 'The temperature's come right down,' he said. 'Anyone can see you're out of the wood.'

'Blanchard told me I'd been poisoned,' Kemp said.

'He told you *what*?'

'He said somebody had probably dropped poison into my food. I mentioned it to the doctor here, and he took it very badly.'

'Well, he would, wouldn't he? You were calling his competence into question.'

'I wasn't. This was before he told me what I was suffering from. He seemed to take it as an insult to his country.'

'They're like that,' Craddock said. 'Anyway Blanchard is the last man whose opinion I put any faith in, even in medical matters. He imagines things. He's been out here too long. They ought to send him home.'

'The main thing in his favour is he'll turn out at night. He certainly uses his imagination. His idea seems to have been that I was having an affair with the Filipino girl who works for me, and I'd upset her and this was her way of getting her own back.'

'Blanchard needs his head examined.'

'He probably does. One slightly worrying thing comes out of this. Mike Jolly is looking after the villa for me, and when I rang him today to see how things were, he told me she hadn't been back.'

Chapter Six

'Mr Kemp, your visit has given great pleasure to us all,' Dr Ahmed said. He had appeared, crisp and bland as if for an important television interview, at the head of a smiling muster of doctors and nurses who had come to say goodbye, and join in a valedictory toast of alcohol-free 'Jamaica Supreme' served foaming in champagne glasses, its sourish, dessert-apple flavour believed by the Arabs almost exactly to copy that of Veuve Clicquot, extra-sec.

The occasion was cheerful but slightly formal, with Dr Ahmed's staff stiffened a little by his presence, as if on parade. A few words seemed called for. 'Thank you all for giving me such a wonderful time,' Kemp said. 'I've caught up with my reading, I've been encouraged to over-eat, and I've slept like a child. The problem now is going to be how to re-adapt to the outside world.'

Dr Ahmed sipped cautiously through persistent froth, then put down his glass. 'We exist like village people here, absorbed in our small affairs. It has been very enlightening to be able to exchange ideas with someone who has seen so much of the world. Having met you in person we shall look forward more than ever to reading your despatches from our country.'

He still lives in hope of something, Kemp decided. He hasn't given up. On a second evening visit to his room the doctor's manner had remained genial and friendly and they had talked about life in England, which Dr Ahmed said it was his ambition to visit. There had been no reference to the overture made on the first occasion. 'I hope we may remain in contact,' the doctor said. 'That is my dearest wish.'

They all trooped out again, but Kemp was able to catch Dr Abd Er Rahman in the corridor. 'What happened to the nurse from Beirut?' he asked. 'I must say goodbye to her.'

'The beautiful Leila, hah? Mr Kemp, you made a great impression on her. She talks of you all the time. This morning she has been called to intensive care. They have a life-support machine which she was required to operate in an emergency. You will find the unit on the top floor. Please go there.'

Kemp took the lift to the top floor, and was shown to the staff room of the intensive care unit, where the atmosphere throbbed with crisis. For ten minutes he got in the way of harassed nurses, finding himself the object of glances, like a tourist who has stumbled unawares into the holy place of an exclusive religion. A nurse who could have been in charge glared at him.

He was much relieved when Leila came through a door. She was wearing a white coat, and her hair had been drawn back under an operating cap. For a moment he was abashed by what might have been professional aloofness, and found himself tongue-tied and awkward.

She walked towards him smiling, and Kemp, who had half-raised his hand, let it drop to his side again, feeling sure that contact of any kind was taboo in this sterilized setting. 'I'm on my way,' he said. 'I do hope this isn't prohibited territory. Had to say goodbye.'

'Going so soon? I'd no idea.'

'They wanted me to stay until the end of the week, but there was some urgent business to be attended to, and I felt a bit of a fraud.'

She was clearly disappointed. 'I looked out all my old pictures of Beirut to show you, including one of the tree. And now you're going.'

'I suppose I can still see them, can't I?'

'If you wish, yes of course. Would you like me to leave them at the reception?'

'No, I wouldn't like that. I'd like you to show me them yourself, and tell me what they're all about. Can't I come back some time when you're off duty?'

'Oh yes. Please do that.'

'When?'

'I'm off afternoons this week. Any afternoon.' Even the cool starchiness of her uniform could not suppress her warmth. He felt encouraged.

'Would there be any hope of my taking you for a run in the car for an hour or two? Perhaps that would be too much for the restrictions?'

She laughed. 'I'm almost a prisoner, but not quite.'

Kemp felt the resentful stare of the supposed sister-in-charge as she crackled past.

'A run in your car would be a lovely idea.'

'Could we make it tomorrow?'

'I don't see why we shouldn't.'

'How long would you be off?'

'Four hours,' she said. 'From two-thirty to six-thirty. I have to be on call again at seven.'

'Marvellous,' he said. 'We could go to Sabratha if you like. Leptis would be too far.'

'Anywhere,' she said. 'Anywhere would be wonderful.' She sounded as if she meant it.

Chapter Seven

Kemp had got the idea of Sabratha from the lady accountant who, determined to get the most out of her stay in the country, had provided herself with a Guide Bleu to the region before her arrival. She was impressed to find that Kemp should be so knowledgeable on the subject of the ruins, and his popularity, which had slumped sharply after he had proposed to make love to her in a labyrinth constructed from lengths of oil pipe and patrolled by guard dogs, staged a sharp recovery.

They drove there to find that autumn had come in a single day, emptying its colours into the burned-out landscape of summer. Brilliant winged insects in migration fluttered over the golden sandstone of the ruins, and the first cold currents veined the sea.

'Picnic first, or sight-seeing first?' Kemp asked.

'Sight-seeing first.'

'Why don't we just wander about and take in what we feel like?' he suggested. 'I brought a guide book just in case, but I don't think we really need it.'

'We'll do anything you like,' she said. 'A few hours of freedom is all that matters to me. This is a wonderful place.'

She took off her shoes, ran barefoot up a monumental staircase leading to nowhere, and did a few steps, arms twisting and hips swaying, of a mock oriental dance on the flat top. Then she came down again, laughing. 'The sea's just over there,' she said. 'You can hear it. Let's go for a walk along the shore and look at the ruins at the same time.'

'Good idea,' he said.

Kemp would have led the way in that direction in any case, knowing that the beauty of what was left of Sabratha lay spread out by the water's edge. In this maritime setting the ruins took on a special vivacity, aglow in the sunlight against the almost menacing darkness of the sea from which they seemed to have drawn all the colour. First came the Temple of Isis, and then the Temple of Liber Pater, endowed and ennobled with the peculiar beauty of time-worn marble; so all these columns, now supporting nothing but the sky, had become separated from any purpose they had served, admirable objects in their own right. Many of them had shed their capitals, and sea-birds had dropped shells here to crack them, leaving the pavement all round littered with tiny shards of mother-of-pearl. 'What's that noise?' Leila asked. He listened to the distant cough of water trapped in half-submerged caves. 'The sea clearing its throat,' he said. They both laughed. Springtime in autumn, he thought. A beautiful occasion in all.

They found themselves in the theatre, a collector's piece—as Kemp always thought of it—among ruins, this stark yet grandiose presence dominating a panorama of so many undecipherable remains. Shadows like enormous birds flew across the three arcaded stories of the great stage house. It was startlingly intact, hard to believe that eighteen centuries had passed since actors presented themselves at its openings and windows. 'I can't believe it isn't a modern copy,' Leila said. But it wasn't.

They inspected the marble reliefs along the stage front that the despoilers and fanatics of history had somehow contrived to overlook, the gods, graces and satyrs, the tragic and comic masks, and it was here, overlooked by the faces of antiquity that they decided to picnic. The Tuesday Hypermarket had supplied Rumanian caviare, to be spread on gritty village bread and washed down with Mike's beer made from Bio-Malt. Studying her, it seemed to Kemp that Leila's features had become more sharply angled and poignant in this classical environment. It was a meal, they agreed, that epitomized their lives in this country.

The pictures of Beirut were admired, wondered at, put away. 'This,' she said, speaking of Sabratha, 'is paradise.'

Gaiety and the spirit of truancy seemed to flow from her. This was no more an outing by the sea. It was an escape. Kemp squeezed her arm with caution, feeling the excitement, the inebriation after a month or so of celibacy, of contact with the mysterious novelty of an unknown female body.

'I didn't tell you how lucky I was to get away.'

'No, you didn't. How was that?'

'Sister Dobrovic, who's in charge of intensive care, was very difficult.'

'But it was your afternoon off, wasn't it?'

'She's acting vice-matron, and what she says goes. You must have seen her when you came to say goodbye.'

'I noticed one of the nurses looking at me as if she wanted to chew my arm off. What's her trouble?'

'Jealousy. Intensive care is very hard work, and she was upset when Dr Ahmed took me off the ward for a week to look after you.'

'I had no idea that happened. What made him do that?'

'The Malaysian sister on your floor didn't speak English very well. I think he wanted to make a good impression on you.'

'I can't imagine why. Pity the acting vice-matron took it to heart.'

'She was ready for me today when I asked for permission to go out with you. She said that as I was a national I came under Muslim laws whether I was a Muslim or not, and that meant I was not allowed to be alone with any male outside the hospital building. It's true, but it's something they turn a blind eye to if they want to. In the end I went to Dr Ahmed about it, and she had to give in. I still had to go through the whole business of signing the Leave of Absence book and writing in your name and telephone number. All to be able to get away for four hours.'

'She's a Yugoslav, isn't she, with that name? They can be very intense. What made you change your nationality?'

'It was automatic. I married a Libyan student I met in Beirut.'

Kemp felt his spirits dip, then criticized himself for being unreasonable. It had come as a slight shock to him that she should have made no mention of a husband until this. But why? What did he expect? Was every girl he met supposed to have kept herself intact until he came on the scene? 'Where's your husband?' he asked.

'He's dead,' she said. 'The marriage lasted three weeks. They drafted him into the army and set him to Uganda, and he was killed in action.'

He shook his head in silence. After an hour of adolescent fantasy he was back in the realism of the local climate. Death from atrocious causes of many kind was a commonplace of the third world, and no emotional iron curtain separated the living from the dead. Kemp had visited a tribe in the interior where the most ecstatically celebrated feast in any man's life was 'the trial for size' when, attended by all his rejoicing relatives and friends, a man lay for a few minutes in the coffin for which they had all clubbed together to buy him. In this atmosphere mourning was little more than a brief ritual, and grief was put aside as easily as love.

'There was a hole in my life,' she said, smiling, 'but now it's closed over. They have a custom in Beirut; the neighbours tie your hands to stop you from killing yourself. You scream, you bite your lips, and you roll on the ground, and then you get up and make tea. Here they are already more civilized.'

Filled with a sudden urgency, Kemp drew her down beside him. He had planned to take her back to the villa if things promised well, then had had second thoughts about this. The neighbours remained invisible, but he knew that there would be an eye at every lattice when the car drew up, and by thus arriving with a woman, blatantly and in broad daylight, he risked scandal.

They kissed and Kemp fondled her limbs cautiously. Accustomed to the bulkier, softer flesh of older women, the almost boyish firmnness of her body came as a surprise. So tight skinned, so smooth, so fragrant, he thought. How many years had passed since he had loved a girl in the flower of her youth? There was no token even of resistance, so why delay? Past experience had shown that few places could be more private than the ruins of Sabratha, defended from intrusion by the native fear of multitudinous ghosts.

They rolled over together, mouths joined, then suddenly she stiffened, cried out and pushed him away. Somewhere behind him and over his head Kemp heard a sound like a gasp, then a scutter of dislodged stones. He scrambled to his feet to see a man hunched like an ape, not twenty feet from them, his eyes staring from a contorted face. The man straightened himself, turned and ran, and Kemp picked up a lump of marble, raised his arm to throw it, then tossed it away. 'A shepherd,' he told her. 'I'm sorry. Very sorry. I think we should go away from here.'

She was amazed by the villa's size. 'It's enormous, isn't it?'

'An Italian general built it back in the thirties when this was their favourite colony. The idea was to copy the Temple of Serapias, but he ran out of cash.'

'Can I see all of it?' she said.

She inspected every room, examining all its contents: the few sticks of utility furniture provided by the landlord and the out-of-focus, hand-tinted photographs in tortoiseshell frames, relics of the General's days. He followed her into the bathroom where the sight of his dressing gown over the back of a chair and his slippers left where he had flung them in a corner reminded him that the Filipino girl had never come back. A strange business, he thought. Very strange. He must try to find out what had become of her.

The door of the wall cupboard where he kept his shaving gear was open. Kemp stood behind her and their eyes met in the mirror.

'Do you live in this big place all by yourself?' she asked.

'So far,' he said. 'I've only been here a matter of weeks. Before that I shared a house with another man.'

'They must like you to give you a place like this, when so many people have to share a room.'

'I do part-time work for one of the ministries. They treat

me pretty well.'

'Yes, they do,' she said. 'Dr Ahmed said you had to have the best of everything. Are you married?'

'I have a wife in England.'

'Why isn't she out here?'

'She leads her life and I lead mine. We used to be together in places like Paris and Cairo. After that she decided she preferred England, and she wanted to stay at home and look after the children. I go back for two or three months every second year.'

'Don't you find it a lonely life?'

'It could be,' he said. 'I have a fairly wide circle of acquaintances.'

She narrowed her eyes in a knowing smile. 'No girlfriends in the background anywhere?'

'At this moment, no.'

'Why don't you have one?'

'They're in short supply. Any woman here on her own can pick and choose.'

'But it hasn't been like that in Beirut, and the other places you've been in?'

'No,' he said. 'It wasn't the same in Beirut, and the other places. Not quite, anyway. This is very monastic by comparison.'

'So it's a matter of opportunity,' she said.

'Opportunity comes into it. I'm only human.'

'Is it a very big part?'

He thought about the problems of opportunity and selection. 'I don't know. It's hard to say. Say half and half.'

'You're very sincere. That's the first thing I decided about you. It's something that appeals to me. So you like women?'

'That should be obvious,' he said.

'And I like men. But I don't care much for expatriates. They bore me with their bridge and all their silly parties.'

'They have to find ways of using up the time,' Kemp said. 'Besides which it's a kind of defence mechanism. It helps draw them together. I'm obliged to give a house-warming party myself in a few days time, and I hope you'll come to it.'

'No,' she said. 'I won't come to your party. You're frank and I'm frank. If I come to your house I don't need the excuse of a party. It will be for you, and not for people who come here to play silly games and get drunk.'

'But you'll come anyway?'

Thinking about it, her expression was quite serious. 'Yes, I probably will. I'll come anyway.'

She had wandered off. 'What's this room?' she asked.

'My bedroom. It's in a bit of a mess.'

He followed her into the room. They sat down on the bed in the dim, diffused light spread from the closed shutters. Kemp felt his mouth dry. He followed the contours of her arm and neck with the tips of his fingers. Her skin felt as cold as marble.

'I've thought about you,' she said, 'and decided we're very much alike. We've both learned not to feel deeply any more. It's a luxury we can't afford. That means we don't have to play games with each other. We've both lost our roots. We both live for the moment. We're free agents. No bad involvements. We kiss and forget. Do you agree?'

'I have to,' he said. 'Don't you ever think of trying to put down new roots?'

'No,' she said. 'I'm resigned, and I prefer it this way. Our Lebanese proverb says, "all that pleases in life is a brief dream". I accept that, and that's the way I want to leave it. So you've been warned.'

She took off her dress. 'We have one hour left,' she said.

Kemp went to the window, and eased open the shutter, fanning light into the room. As he did so the shutter on a window at the same level in the admiral's house across the road banged to. He turned back to the alabaster of Leila's naked body on the bed.

Chapter Eight

Kemp tore open the letter from Claire, which he knew would contain little for his comfort. It had been written only two days previously and carried by an expatriate returning from leave. He skimmed quickly through the three pages, expertly sifting the hard news from matters of less consequence.

I've just been having a long chat with Teddy Vickers, who has proved once again to be such a good friend. The sale of the house fell through as we knew it would, the market being what it is. Nobody wants to look at such a barn of a place that needs so much doing to it. Teddy's suggestion was that I should convert part to furnished rooms for letting to students, for which there is always a demand. The cost would be in the region of £20,000 and would give me six rooms lettable at about £20 each per week. Teddy actually offered to lend us half this if you could find the balance, but must have an early decision, so please phone him. If we could take him up on this it would make all the difference in the world to the financial situation.'

But why? Why should this be? he asked himself. Kemp paid out conscience money endlessly without complaint, five hundred here and a thousand there at each new hint of reproach. It had been an absurdity to keep on the house at a time when it could have been sold. 'The boys had to have somewhere to call their home,' she said, with her customary skill in shifting the responsibility for her wishes to other shoulders. Surely, he had thought, three up and two down in a good tree-lined suburban street would have been acceptable to them?

'The news of the boys is as good as ever. I can't begin to tell you how much school has done for them. They take everything in their stride. We had a happy holiday together and only wished you could have been with us. Whatever sacrifices we made, I'm sure it was right.'

He re-read the letter, which was along the usual lines of communications from Claire, although worse this time than expected. It was a relief that she had calmly accepted his news that he had put off his home trip for six months. 'Sorry we shan't be seeing you until the spring,' she said, and left it at that.

As for the great, costly white elephant of their Oxford house, it was at the root of so many of their troubles, the monstrous encumbrance that punished him with its decay, with its dry rot, its sagging roof, its bulging walls that sopped up damp like a sponge, its faulty wiring and cracked drains. It was unnecessarily close to the colleges, with a view of dreaming spires and a landscaped garden full of rare shrubs which did not interest him in the slightest, and it cost a fortune to keep up. While not an extravagant woman Claire seemed blind to the necessity of cutting costs and had a knack of making him feel mean whenever he suggested that cuts could be made. She still drove a Volvo estate in Oxford's cluttered streets when a baby Renault would have been both cheaper and handier. The big car made her feel safe, she said.

Kemp wanted to put off any decision on the matter of the house, so he delayed calling Vickers, and in the end Vickers called him. 'I tried to get you a couple of times, but no reply.'

'I've been away for a few days,' Kemp said.

'It was largely to thank you for that report on the attacks on private traders. Marvellous stuff. It's the way they all go in the end. Do you happen to have heard from Claire?'

'Yes, I have, and thank you for your magnificent offer.'

'How do you feel about it?'

'Well, naturally, I'm more than grateful, but I couldn't dream of accepting it. Apart from which, my trouble at this moment is that I'm paying fourteen and a half percent on an overdraft.'

'Sincerely, Ron, you ought to do something about that house. And about Claire. Did she tell you she'd lost her job?' Claire had been employed on a part-time basis in an Oxford bookshop.

'She didn't. That's bad news, because little as they paid her, it gave her an interest. She tends not to tell me these things.'

'She doesn't want to worry you.'

'I know that. It's a problem, and quite honestly I don't know what to do about it. About the house, I mean. I must have spent five or six thousand on it in the past couple of years.'

'Nothing you could flog, I suppose, to raise some cash?'

'The boat, but it's the wrong time of the year. There aren't any buyers about until the spring.'

'Could you cut down in some way on the boys?'

'I'd do so willingly. I'm all in favour of comprehensives but Claire wouldn't hear of it. You should know her by now.'

'Well it's a pity. I just had this small windfall, and I'd have liked to be able to help out.'

'I know you would, Teddy, and I can't tell you how much I appreciate it. Listen, give me a few days to think about it. There is a chance of being able to do something, but it's so remote I don't even want to talk about it at this stage. Give me a day or two to mull it over in my mind.'

Within five minutes of Kemp hanging up, Vickers was through to Jimson in Malta. 'I have the impression we're getting somewhere,' he said. 'I've known the man quite a long time, and things always take a little time to sink in. Nothing really to go on yet, but the signs are he's weakening.'

'It happens so often,' Jimson said. 'They nearly go through the roof when you put a proposition, after which they calm down and begin to take a rational view. Perhaps I should try to have another word with him myself. Anyway, we live in hope.'

Chapter Nine

Salim wanted to see Kemp about a meeting he had just had with the Minister.

'He is very pleased with the newspaper's success under your guidance, and he has asked if you have any objection to the publication of a story concerning yourself?'

'None whatever.'

'You recall your story of your grandfather's association with the Sultanate of Mahir? Could reference be made to that?'

'I don't see why not.'

Kemp's grandfather, a natural opportunist employed in the Colonial Service shortly after the first World War, had been lent as adviser to the Sultan of Mahir in Southern Arabia, soon becoming the power behind the scenes. Preparing to assume open control his grandfather had left the service, only to be foiled by the Government's prompt invitation to the Sultan to come to London, where he was given a knighthood and a pension, while his state was incorporated in the Protectorate. As inheritor of the family opportunism, the lessons in this misadventure were not lost on Kemp.

'I think your readers might be interested,' Kemp said. 'It's a strange little story. How an Englishman set out to serve the Arab people, and how he came to a sad end.'

Salim had a favour to ask. The Minister had also requested a report on the tomato-growing project at Benghazi. Could he go there?

'I'd be delighted to help, but why me?'

'Because we cannot rely as well as we would wish on the objectivity of our own people. In the hope that you would acquiesce I have booked a seat for you on the afternoon plane.

Please excuse the short notice. The planes are very heavily booked. I trust that this is convenient?'

'Benghazi isn't precisely my favourite city, Salim, but I'll do it for you with pleasure. I couldn't get back tonight, I suppose?'

'That is impossible. I have also taken the liberty of reserving a room in the Maghreb Hotel, and a seat on the plane returning tomorrow morning.'

'Right. I'll go and take a shufti at what the project has to offer, and report back to you tomorrow afternoon. Inshallah.'

Kemp next tried to ring Leila at the hospital, a gross self-indulgence as he knew in view of what he had seen of the pressure of work in the ward. The operator agreed with what seemed reluctance to put him through to intensive care, and the nurse taking the call who, from the curtness of her tone, he was sure could be none other than Sister Dobrovic, asked him to repeat his name, then left him holding on for what seemed a long time. He was about to hang up and dial again when she was back, to ask him what she called the nature of his business. Her voice held both impatience, and severity.

'It's a personal friend. She's expecting me to call. I'm sorry to bother you in this way.'

'Our rules are that nurses are not permitted to speak on the telephone on private affairs when they are on duty in the wards. At this time she is in the theatre. She cannot speak.'

'I'd like to leave a message to say I'll ring later when she's off duty.'

'There is no way of telling when that may be. We are very busy.'

'All I wanted to say is that I shall be away in the country for a couple of days, and I will contact her when I get back. I'd be most grateful.'

For the third time there was a pause before Sister Dobrovic—if it were she—spoke, preceded by that special audial vacuum produced when a hand is clapped lightly over the mouthpiece of the receiver.

'If I can pass a message to her, I will do so,' she said.

Kemp found something a little disturbing about this episode. He had a feeling that someone had been standing at the sister's side monitoring the conversation, and instructing her replies. He tried unsuccessfully to dismiss this fancy from his mind. The Benghazi plane took off at 3.20 p.m., and shortly before three he made a further attempt, assuming that by this time Leila would be off duty, to contact her in the nurses' quarters. But she was not to be found.

Benghazi was a place Kemp visited as infrequently as he could, a mess of a town swirling with brick dust and exhaust fumes, glutted with bewildered camels and thundering juggernauts, with a north wind too often shrieking through the girders of unfinished buildings, girls in uniform stamping up and down the old promenade, and excavators penetrating the narrowest of lanes in search of new terrain where holes in the earth could be opened.

Kemp took a taxi from the airport across town to the project. He found himself in a hangar like an iron church, full of shallow tanks containing the liquid in which the tomatoes were encouraged to grow. A few sodden, dejected plants showed no intention of producing fruit, and two Arabs with holy wonder in their faces presented a tray containing eleven tomatoes, like priests in the Cathedral of Naples exhibiting a miraculous liquefaction of blood. This, as far as he could gather, was the production for the week so far. The scheme was the brain-child of East German technologists, who had failed to inject any enthusiasm into the Arabs operating a process which appeared to fly in the face of nature and the designs of God. Driving back to the town's centre, Kemp passed fields growing magnificent vegetables of all descriptions. He knew that their owners were destined to become the next victims of scientific technology, soon to be moved off their land into projects like the one he had just visited.

The only reason anybody in their right mind wanted to go to Benghazi was to pick up a Misurata carpet in the souk. In their bold, archaic surrealism no two examples were alike, and as no way had been found of adapting their manufacture to mass-production and the computerized loom, the rumour was they would soon cease to exist. It occurred to Kemp that if ever he was to buy a Misurata, now was the time. As soon as he had checked in at the Maghreb, he walked across to what was left of the souk, bought a carpet from the only dealer still in the business, and departed.

The plane left at seven in the morning, and Kemp, arriving at the airport at six, found that not only was his plane overbooked, but at the centre of a riot. One of the inconveniences to which visitors to Benghazi were exposed was their involvement in the stampede down the narrow and dangerous passage known as 'the tube' leading from the departure lounge to the planes about to take off. Announcements over the loudspeakers, given in Arabic, were normally incomprehensible even to the Arabs themselves, and since no one could understand what flight was being called, every muffled roar from the speakers precipitated a rush of up to five hundred travellers into the tube, where they were trapped by the gates at the further end. The chaos was aggravated on this particular morning by a series of battles between jealous husbands and other males whom they claimed had taken advantage of the confusion in the tube to fondle their wives.

Kemp, arriving at the height of the uproar, just as police, whirling their batons, charged into the tube, knew that he would not be travelling that day. Nor did it seem that there was much hope of getting away on the following day, as the flight was fully booked, and the wait-list closed. His predicament turned out to be all the more acute when he was told at the hotel that delegations had arrived to occupy every room together with every square yard of unutilized space where makeshift bedding could be put down in emergency.

He went back to take the advice of the man from whom he had bought the carpet. 'I have to get back to Tripoli by road. Anybody you know going?'

'My brother-in-law will be driving his truck there today. He will take you.' The carpet seller had been a lad of eighteen in 1943 when the Eighth Army had rolled into Benghazi and had happy memories of a lively business with the troops, exchanging fresh eggs for guaranteed once-only used tea leaves. In spite of its miserable amenities, Britons condemned to live in Benghazi still had a head start over the rest of the expatriates.

An hour later Kemp was seated at the brother-in-law's side in the air-conditioned cabin of a Mercedes lorry bound for Tripoli, 600 miles away. Mohammed the driver said that should God shower them with his mercies the journey could be accomplished in ten hours, but Kemp knew from his tone—the submissive monotone of a man rattling through a prayer—that this was unlikely. Mohammed, too, liked the English, happy to have been swindled by them in the old days, in the trade for the dregs of British teapots. Three wilted-looking teenage lads squatted in the back of the lorry. They were being taken to Tripoli where a doctor could be bribed to issue them with certificates stating that they suffered from heart disease, and thus were unsuitable for military service. This would cost a thousand dinars. The driver laughed in a heart-broken way. 'Once it was good to have sons. Now better girls.'

The Mercedes pounded westwards over a road that had taken unending punishment from the transporters burdened with steel for the rigs. In places it was cracked and fissured as if by a Richter scale-five earthquake. In others it had been pounded to dust. Inland a gunmetal desert was laid out under a sky wearing a chainmail of hard little clouds. The desert was strewn with abandoned machinery, built up and shaped by drifting sand like the burial mounds of Celtic chieftains. Kemp was unhappy about the slow time they were making, irritated by the delays, nervous and anxious to be back. 'Are we going to make it?' he asked.

'Inshallah,' the driver said. He smiled with the secret knowledge of impending defeat.

They crashed through the wide main streets of Ghemines, of Adjabia, and of Brega, over concrete surfaces patched with the fur of animals that had not understood that the age of the horse-drawn vehicle was no more. In Argheila, Kemp could not restrain himself any longer from calling the hospital.

The usual glittering hypermarket dominated the cataclysm of development in this town. Kemp left Mohammed and his sons to brew their tea in the car-park, pestered by a camel in rut that had taken the Mercedes for a female of its kind and was drooling over the bodywork with its saliva, while he went into the market to phone.

He stood with his head and torso wedged in something like a space-man's suit, dialled, got through instantly, and was connected without demur or delay with Leila's extension in the staff quarters. For once in this country where an excellent telephone service was provided, the connection was poor, a circumstance causing him to wonder, jumpily, if someone could be listening in on the line.

'It's you? You sound such a long way away,' she said.

'Terrible connection,' he said. 'Did you get my message? I'm in Argheila.'

'Argheila?' It sounded like a thin echo of his own voice, in a vast empty room.

'Half-way from Benghazi. Couldn't get on the plane, so I'm on my way back by road.'

A crackle of static carried half a sentence away '. . . as soon as you can,' she said.

'I can't hear you. Can you hear me?'

'I can hear you. I'm in trouble. When will you be back?'

'After midnight. Tomorrow morning latest. For God's sake what's wrong?'

'I'll tell you about it.'

'Can't you speak now?'

'Not now.'

'Very bad, is it?'

'Bad, get back soon.'

'Could be very late tonight. More likely tomorrow.'

Her voice wavered away. 'Can't explain ... ring me ... when you can.'

Esider, Ben Javad, Sultan, Sirte; the lacklustre towns were marked on the long slow curve of the coast like the hours on a clock that was running down. Their average speed dropped from fifty miles an hour, to forty, then thirty. The paved road split into slivers of cracked macadam, and they were diverted into a desert of carboniferous grit full of the swaying, mourning figures of black whirlwinds. Cars and trucks, lights on, hurtled in all directions, charging at each other head-on, then swerving away at the last split second to avoid collision.

'Are we going to make it, Mohammed?'

'Inshallah, sir. The road is very bad, and I think the truck is tired.'

The Mercedes was losing power, overheating, its engine beginning to miss. At about six with the last of the sunlight drawn back like a quilt from the high dunes, and the desert as grey as a corpse, Mohammed pulled off the road and stopped. 'Now we have no light. We must stay here tonight.'

The three unsmiling sons, moving as slowly as if they had convinced themselves that they were really about to suffer coronaries, began a slow search of the neighbourhood for dead acacia branches to make a fire. For the third time that day they brewed a pot of tea, then within minutes an enormous steel-plated vehicle slid into sight round a bend in the road. A thousand horse-power moved it in cushioned silence on its twelve wheels. The great gun thrust from a turret in front rocked smoothly from side to side as if to sniff out the trail of scent laid ahead, while a double row of rocket-launchers was banked on each side. It slowed, swung round in its cape of shadow, with the delicate certainty of a fighting bull turning on its small hooves. It stopped, and a machine-gun jutting from a small, square embrasure, made a fractional adjustment to hold them in its sights. Kemp felt that it had sensed their presence there as if by instinct. A hatch popped open, and an army officer in a black track-suit lifted himself out and dropped to the ground. He inspected them, smiling absently, with a pair of wide-aperture night-glasses at a range of thirty yards, while Kemp and Mohammed pretended to talk to each other about the prospects of repairing the lorry and the three sickly sons sat hunched over their cups. Then the officer went back to the armoured car, and climbed in, and it went off, with a great surge of acceleration and a backlash of small stones from the road's unfinished surface.

'What was that, Mohammed?'

'Flying patrol, sir. For keeping watch on coast.'

'What are they looking for?'

'That is something we cannot know. All we know is what they say in the bazaar. The Colonel has many enemies. They say that at the time of the Aïd there was an attack on his life, and that mujahadin will be sent to kill him.'

'You seemed nervous.'

'I am afraid this man take my sons.'

'They're likely to do that, are they?'

'If they are short of soldiers they will take anyone they can find.'

The fire died down and the desert chill rose up out of the stones. They slept in the back of the lorry, and by dawn Mohammed was at work tracking down electrical faults.

'How long, Mohammed?'

'Now is finished. Please to get in. If no more troubles, inshallah we shall arrive by half-day.'

The rest of the journey was trouble-free, but nerve-rackingly slow, and it was five in the afternoon before Mohammed dropped Kemp off at the Green Mosque. He rang Leila. 'Come now,' she said. 'It may be difficult to talk.'

He took a taxi to the hospital where she was waiting for him, dressed in her ordinary street clothes in the nurses' sitting room. She seemed held in suspense, like a patient in a waiting room, alert through the slow ticking-away of time for the buzzer that would summon her to the doctor's presence to discuss a serious condition. A small, tight, unflinching smile put a brave front on disastrous news that was to come. The room had been garnished with enormous Amazonian plants, and they took refuge in a corner smelling of the jungle, curtained by the aerial roots of the largest monstera he had ever seen. 'There's been an awful scandal,' she told him. 'Another girl and I have been suspended from duty.'

'Good God.'

Two probationers turned the corner of their arbour, to shoot curious glances at them as they passed in step. Leila drew her chair closer to his. 'There was a check on the D.D.A. cupboard in intensive care, and they found some drugs missing.'

'How do you come into it?'

'It's supposed to have happened when I was on duty last time. Someone helped themselves to diamorphine and pethadine.'

'Are they able to say exactly when this was done? Aren't drugs being used all the time?'

'Yes, but it has to be written up in the register. When any drug is taken from the cupboard the details of the case and the quantity of the drug used have to be put in the book. I was on duty with Nurse Martínez and we both checked the drugs against the register and signed for them when we took over. When the next shift came on they found there were shortages.'

'Could anyone help themselves while your back was turned?'

'No, because the cupboard has an inner door, and each of the nurses on duty has a key to one door. It works like a bank safe-deposit.'

A covey of nurses clacked past them over the mosaic floor on their way to report for duty. They wore smartly cut pink and grey uniforms with miniature Victorian-style capes of the kind once prim, but now chic. Leila had turned her face away at their approach, and her chin was trembling.

'Supposing a key got lost? How would you open the cupboard?'

'They have duplicate keys.'

'And where are they kept?'

'In the Director's office.'

'Then that's the answer. Somebody got hold of the duplicate keys. Tell me exactly what happened when this loss was discovered.'

'Nurse Martínez and I went to the staff room to hand over to Sister Dobrovic and Nurse Beck who were coming on. We found that Dr Ahmed was with them.'

'Had he ever turned up before to check the cupboard in person?'

'Not so far as I know. Dr Ahmed told us to unlock the cupboard, and then went through the stock, item by item, and checked it against the register.'

'Which suggests that they expected to find what they found. How did Dr Ahmed take it? Was there any sort of outburst?'

'He was as calm as he always is. He could have been complaining that somebody had forgotten to enter up a patient's temperature chart.'

'He's a very controlled man. Now let's suppose you were set up in some way. Could Nurse Martínez have come into it?'

'It's out of the question. She's a wonderful person.'

'How about Sister Dobrovic, then? She doesn't like you. She's probably jealous of you, but would she really go to such lengths to ruin your career—to say nothing of Nurse Martínez's career?'

'I can't believe it.'

'We're left with Dr Ahmed. From all you've told me he seems to have been well enough disposed towards you. In any case he's too big a man to stoop to this kind of meanness. Wouldn't you have said that?'

'Yes, I would.'

'The mystery remains,' Kemp said. 'So what's the situation now?'

'Nurse Martínez and I have been suspended pending investigation.'

'And how long will that take?'

'About a week.'

'So what do we do?'

'I want to get away. I want to go now.'

'Yes,' he said, stroking her hands. 'I know you do.'

'I'm under a cloud. They can talk of nothing else in the hospital, and it's easy to see that everybody takes it for granted that we're guilty.'

'But could you simply get up and walk out?'

'No, I couldn't. In the first place I'd be running away, and secondly I wouldn't be allowed to break my contract. We haven't been accused of anything. Drugs that Nurse Martínez and I were responsible for are missing, and the case is being investigated by the governing board. That's how it is.'

'Supposing it goes against you?'

'We'd be dismissed.'

'There's only one thing we can do,' Kemp said. 'Wait and see. In the meanwhile, since you're suspended from duty, I can't see that the hospital has any jurisdiction over you.'

'I don't know. I've no way of knowing how I stand. Nurse Martínez took the law into her own hands and went to stay with friends.'

'That's the answer then,' he said. 'I want you to come home with me. If Nurse Martínez can walk out on them so can you.'

'Her friends are an elderly couple.'

'Does that make all the difference?'

'She can't be accused of misconduct. No woman here is free to come and go as she pleases. We're subservient.'

'Only because you've been taught to believe you are. We went to bed together after our trip to Sabratha. Is there any difference?'

'Yes. The difference was that no one knew.'

'Need they know if you come home with me now?'

'They will know,' she said.

'Does it really matter?'

'While Africa remains Africa it does.'

Refusing to give up, he had taken her into his arms. Then he caught sight of a curious eye watching them through a hole in a monstera leaf. He grimaced angrily and it was withdrawn.

'They'll always be watching,' she said.

Chapter Ten

Kemp went to see Salim, and the tomato-growing project was dismissed in a few sentences. Salim's hands sculpted abstracts of resignation. 'What went wrong? What was missing?'

'Faith,' Kemp told him. 'You people believe that God intended plants to grow in earth, not water.'

'You have had a wasted trip. I am sorry. Once again we have thrown away many thousands of dinars.'

'I'm afraid you have.'

'It would have been so much better for us to have had your advice before this project was started. So very much better.'

'I've seen it happen so often before in developing countries. People get hooked on anything that sounds like advanced technology. The Cubans threw away millions on all sorts of schemes like this, then went back to sugar.'

'Mr Kemp, I'm sorry. Actually I'm also meddling in something that doesn't concern me, another project which is worrying me. Do you know we are to make a trout farm to produce millions of trout per annum?'

'I can't see you making a success of that either. Where's the farm to be?'

'They are altering the lake at Bir Ganem.'

'But that's a salt lake.'

'Their plan is to drain the lake and remove the salt, and refill with fresh water. Trees will be planted to shade the banks, and plants introduced to provide oxygen. You see, we are drowning in sophistication.'

Kemp shook his head in wonderment.

'You do not think this is possible?' Salim asked. 'I can see you do not.'

'Trout flourish in a cold climate,' Kemp said. 'This is

Africa. However fresh the water you start off with, the salt in the earth will pollute it, and the summer temperatures will be too high. If any trout survive, the birds will fish them out.'

'We are at the mercy of foreign specialists,' Salim said. 'It is in their interest that we should agree to take up all these projects. What it is necessary for us to find is an honest man to advise us. Now we are like sheep thrown to the wolves.' Suddenly he was a merchant again, with something to sell. 'Would there be any hope, Mr Kemp—? Could I speak to my superiors and suggest to them that such a man exists? Please forgive me. I do not wish to impose upon you. You have been so kind.'

The breakthrough, Kemp thought. At last his modest involvement with *The Green Standard* seemed about to pay off. It was a moment of cautious triumph. 'Be sure I'd do all I could at any time, Salim. Can't really imagine there's much I have to offer, but for whatever it's worth I'm at your disposal.'

'Well then, that is what I will do,' Salim said, 'and I rejoice in your friendship. Now perhaps I have some small thing to offer in return. The site of the bathing beach has been approved.'

'Good,' Kemp said. 'And are we likely to be able to use it before the weather turns chilly?'

'Oh yes. Oh, I think so. Yes, I am quite sure. Now prepare yourself for a surprise when I tell you the location. First, please guess where this could be.'

'I simply don't know. Near one or more of the big hotels, I suppose.'

'That is out because there is no sand. Only rock. No, the beach is to be located at Kilometre Seven, within sight of your villa. Now I'm sure you are a very pleased man.'

'Naturally I'm pleased, my pleasure only being slightly dimmed by the thought of all those beach parties I'm going to be expected to give.'

'You understand that this in the meanwhile is in great confidence.'

'Of course. When will there be an announcement?'

'I can't say because we must wait for our Ministry of Defence. They are very slow and careful in everything they do. We shall have to wait for their okay. In the meanwhile it would please me if you would look at the position we have chosen, as soon as you can. We should appreciate your suggestions.'

'What sort of suggestions?'

'About what is to be done to make the foreigners enjoy this place. Shall we have a pool with an island and a bridge? A fountain? Maybe some tall, pink wading birds with their wings clipped?'

'Nothing like that,' Kemp said. 'Just a good stretch of beach, free of tar and plastic.'

'You make it very easy for us. When will it be convenient for you to see this site?'

'Whenever you like. Today or tomorrow. Any time.'

'At the moment the beach is being made safe. I will speak to the officer in charge of the clearing and he will come, perhaps tomorrow morning to take you.'

'I'll be waiting for him. And thank you for all your much appreciated efforts, Salim. You've been as kind as you always are.'

'It has been a pleasure.'

'One other thing, Salim. You're a man of the world.'

'Excuse me, of the developing world, ha, ha.'

'Well, it's still the world in my use of the term. The problem is this. As you know, I'm hardly a gay bachelor, but I do like to be able to have the occasional girlfriend round wherever I happen to be living.'

'And why should you not? Who would think worse of you for that?'

'The thing is, I've formed an attachment for a young lady. She may be around quite a bit.'

'I am delighted to hear this. It is good news. It is not good for any man to live alone.'

'How do I stand with the neighbours?'

'They are sophisticated persons, who accept that because of our customs many of us are still living in the past. You are a friend. Every allowance will be made for you. Is this happy lady British?'

'No.' Kemp hoped that Salim would leave it at that.

'Unhappily we have very few British or American ladies in our country. There are many from Eastern Europe. They have a good education, I think. Some of them speak many languages. Arabic too. That is an accomplishment.'

'The lady in question is one of your nationals.'

Salim seemed to flinch, as if taken by surprise by one of his electrically shiftable pieces of furniture that had moved of its own accord. 'This could be complicated,' he said. 'Ladies of so many races are to be found in our city, it would have been easier to make a different choice.'

Kemp raised his hands, palms outwards, in a common gesture he had picked up to express submission to the divine will. 'These things are decided elsewhere.'

'You are becoming like us. You are blaming God for your mistakes,' Salim said.

'Before we go any further, the young lady doesn't happen to be a Muslim.'

'It makes no difference. If she is one of our nationals she is treated in the same way.'

'Do you happen to know what are the problems involved?'

'The problem is with the law. It has been changed. Only three of our local ladies have married foreigners, one of these being my own secretary. Last year there was a change in the law. In some ways, I tell you with sorrow, we have become more fanatical. Now such marriages are no longer possible.'

'Has this anything to do with religion?'

'There are many religious people here now, such as preachers from the desert, who oppose foreign ways. The influence of these narrow-minded people is very strong. If a woman marries a foreigner they imagine that this man will come to live with her in one of our villages and he will carry with him such customs as whisky-drinking and the exchange of wives. May I understand that the lady who interests you is not married?'

'No.'

'That is a great relief, because otherwise an association would be dangerous for both. I would not recommend it.'

'And as it is?'

'I am doubtful. This is what I think you call a grey area. Happily you have nothing but friends in this town. If you had an enemy he would find a way to use this against you. If this lady comes into your house it is better that she has a woman companion with her. Then no one will throw stones at your door.'

'Do you mean that literally?' Kemp asked.

'No, not literally, it is an expression to show you the mentality of these backward people.'

'Thank you, Salim,' Kemp said. 'At least I know now what I'm up against.'

'Whatever you have told me will be locked away in my confidence,' Salim said. 'Think carefully on what you must do. Perhaps you will change your mind.'

He got back to the villa in the evening, optimistic on the whole from his meeting with Salim. Leila seemed jittery, and he could find no way to draw her out of herself. 'I thought you would never come,' she said. 'I was afraid to be here by myself.'

'There's absolutely nothing to worry about. I saw this friend at the Ministry today who was responsible for getting the villa for me, and I decided to put it to him.'

'You mean you told him about us?'

'Well, yes. Not mentioning you by name.'

'Or giving him any idea of who I could be?'

'Certainly not.'

'You didn't say I was a nurse?'

'No. We respect each other, and I know he'll keep my confidence. They're obviously very hot on morality, even if not as bad as the Saudis. I told him I had formed an attachment for one of his nationals, and asked him what I ought to do about it. What he said, by and large, was there was nothing really to worry about unless the girl involved happened to be married.'

'Ah.'

'So things aren't really too bad. They make it quite clear that they don't approve of romantic associations with foreigners and they're going to discourage them in any way they can, but you can beat the system. His recommendation was that I could fix up with some woman to move in so long as you're here and act as chaperone. There'd be no difficulty in arranging that since people are having to sleep on the ferries in the harbour.'

'How do you know that the man you've been talking to won't report all you've told him to the police?'

'Because I know him,' Kemp said gently. 'Not only is he a very nice man, but to some extent he depends upon me.'

'They mustn't know at the hospital that I'm here.'

'I thought they knew. Where did you tell them you were going?'

'To stay with Nurse Martínez and her friends. She agreed to cover for me.'

The telephone rang. He reached out and picked up the receiver and the line went dead. It was something that happened often enough on this overloaded urban system, but it set her trembling. He had no sooner hung up when the doorbell went. Kemp got up and went to the window. The moon had risen on a cage of girders of the house they were putting up next to the admiral's across the street, and an abandoned cement mixer looked like a monstrous silver top. A long, shining car had drawn up at his door. 'Don't go down,' she implored. 'Let him ring. He'll go away.'

He tried to laugh her out of her fears. 'It'll be one of my friends,' he said. 'I'll have to go down. They'll see by the car that I'm here.'

It turned out to be a pleasant young Arab brought by a new Mercedes, who had come to the wrong address, and who apologised over and over again for his mistake which was easy enough to make in a street with no numbers.

Kemp went back to Leila. 'Describe him, please. What was

he like?' she wanted to know.

'Just a nice young man with a gold watch and a big car. He was asking for some people who live a few yards up the street.'

'Did you believe him?'

'Why shouldn't I? I'm sure he was genuine enough. I happen to know the people he was asking for by sight. They really exist.'

'Soon somebody will come to the door and ask for somebody else.'

'I doubt it, but even if they do, what does it matter? I explain that they've come to the wrong house and they go away. It's of no importance.'

'You don't understand the way they work,' she said. 'There are spies everywhere in this country.'

'If anybody's really spying on us, they've nothing to gain by going about it like this. All the same I've a suggestion to make. You've been under a great deal of strain and you need taking out of yourself. Rather than staying here waiting for the doorbell to ring, why don't we go out on the town? It's still early.'

'Where would we go?'

'The Mediterranean, for example. They have music tonight.'

She shook her head in renewed alarm. 'I'd never dream of going to a place like that.'

'What's wrong with the Mediterranean? It's free of oilmen and it's usually quiet. We could tuck ourselves away into a nice quiet corner, have a meal, and listen to the music.'

'The waiters would see us together.'

'They'd have to.' He turned it into a dispirited joke. 'Unless we sat at separate tables and made signs to each other.'

'All waiters are police spies. Everybody knows that. They'd put it in their report.'

'What of it? There's no law even in this country against a man taking a girl out for dinner.'

'It would get back to the hospital. How could I be staying with Nurse Martínez and having dinner with you at the Mediterranean?'

'I can't see how one rules the other out. All the same, this is a situation we have to face up to. We have to do something to straighten things out so that you can get over this feeling that we're on the run. Do you see any reason why I shouldn't see Dr Ahmed and ask him to clarify your position vis-à-vis the Hospital?'

'Dr Ahmed. Oh no. I couldn't bear that. Don't do that.'

'He's an intelligent man, with no axe to grind, and I believe I can talk to him. I want someone to explain to me in clear-cut terms just how you stand. As you've been suspended with your future left in a state of limbo, are you or are you not free to lead your life in your own way, and come and go as you please? Does that seem unreasonable?'

'All Dr Ahmed can talk to you about is hospital rules. This is something for the police.'

'You're mistaken. I'm utterly convinced of that. Leaving out Saudi Arabia and Iran, there's no country in the world I know of where it's a criminal offence to go to bed with an unmarried woman, or for an unmarried woman to take a lover. Whatever the mullahs may say, those are the facts.' He was indignant now at the puritans and fanatics who were allowed to spread fear from behind the screen of laws that did not exist.

'I'm frightened,' she said. 'I think I'd like to go back to the hospital if they'll have me.'

Chapter Eleven

The doorbell rang at six. Leila slipped naked from the bed and went to the window to pull back a slat of the Venetian blind and peer down into the street. 'It's a soldier,' she said.

'At this unearthly hour? Oh my God, do they never sleep?'

He got up, put on his clothes, and went down.

A young captain was at the door. He looked like a genial Afghan, with a strikingly hooked nose and handlebar moustache with points reaching almost to his eyes, his face dark against the patched morning sunshine. He was dressed in sharply pressed denim fatigues, worn with what Kemp momentarily took to be an Arsenal supporters' scarf. The Honda motorcycle he had arrived on leaned on its stand. 'You are Mr Kemp?'

'I am.'

'Sir, I am happy to meet you. I have come to show you the beach. Will you please accompany me?'

Kemp sat himself on the pillion of the motorcycle and they rode down a trail twisting through the oleanders at the back of his garden, and then through the tufted hillocks and spiny shrubs of the former no-go zone, to the water's edge.

They got off. The captain propped the bike against the remnant of an anchor, and they walked together to the edge of the sand, where the tide had sketched in a line of wrack, of cuttle bone, shells and weed, in which numerous small land-crabs busied themselves.

'Sir,' said the captain. 'This is the best beach in Tripoli.'

'I know it is,' Kemp said.

'It is for you. We are making this beach clean. I know this beach will please you.'

'There's no doubt whatever about that.'

A great change had overtaken the area since only two evenings before when Kemp had sat looking out to sea from his roof-terrace as he sipped one of Mike Jolly's Bio-Malt beers at sundown. All the buckled oil-drums, the tangled cables, and the rusted piping that had monopolized the view on that occasion were gone, to reveal the sparkle of the finest white shingle, which slid under the water the colour of a kingfisher's wing. Engineers with maps and metal detectors were lifting mines and loading them on trolleys, and the soldiers following them filled in the holes they left with sand, or covered them with rectangles of turf, according to the environment. The army songs they quavered in chorus suggested love-sickness rather than martial fervour.

'This beach will be cleared for you tomorrow, sir,' the captain said. 'The part for you to use will be marked with these tapes we are putting now. Please do not cross these tapes, sir. If you do'—he broke off for a joyful laugh—'you will fly into the air—poof!'

'I'll keep on the right side of the tapes. Be sure of that.'

The Captain was eager to please. 'Sir, there is one thing on this beach that is wrong. There is no shade. You want shade?'

'How can we have shade if there isn't any?'

'We can dig up two trees to bring them here for you. Too much sun is bad for the skin.'

'Don't bother. It's fine as it is.'

'There is no bother. We will bring the palms for you. A diving board you want? An area for sport? Badminton, netball, maybe? You want goalposts?'

'No, not goalposts. I think they'd spoil the view.'

'Cabins for undressing? Showers if you like?'

'Never mind about the cabins and the shower. All we really want is a nice, clean, ordinary beach. And thank you for all your hard work.'

'*Marhaba*, sir, as we say. It is our pleasure.'

Kemp's thoughts had turned to Jimson and his easy money. How easy to have taken it, to have solved all his problems instantly and at a stroke by summoning up the courage to cash in this one and only voucher ever handed him by the goddess of luck. Within a week or so everyone in Tripoli would know all there was to be known about this beach, including all the facts of obvious interest to those who would use it in the matter of oil pollution, the existence of dangerous currents, and the possible prevalence of the stinging jelly-fish known as medusas which abounded in North African inshore waters. Five, six, seven, eight thousand, the numbers ticked off by Jimson with scarcely a shrug of the shoulders, a casual and limitless flux of easy money, of no more importance to some faceless paymaster behind the scenes than the small change in Kemp's pocket. Kemp was tempted to see in this feckless spilling of treasure an inefficiency of the kind that beset oil multinationals, where responsibility could find nowhere to lay its head. A project was presented, they paid out, *and then they forgot*. He suspected now that he could have taken the money, and whatever he offered would have been gobbled up by a computer, to lie undiscovered in its belly for ever. It was a custombuilt situation for La Rochefoucauld's wry maxim, 'It is not the things we have done, but those we failed to do, we regret.'

Thirty yards away a group of fishermen squatted round a transistor radio. They were figures from the Middle Ages, leathery, sun-cured, hawk-faced men, their heads bound up in piratical turbans. A narrow lane through tapes led to the safe area where they were gathered close to their boats. The captain followed Kemp's glance. 'They are very ignorant men, sir. When the beach is ready for you we shall tell them to go away.'

'Don't do that,' Kemp said. 'They add to the charm of the place. Don't see enough real fishermen these days.'

The captain was mystified, but prepared to indulge any foreign whim. 'You want to go talk to them, sir?'

'I'd like to get a closer look at the boats,' Kemp said.

They walked together up a taped-out lane for a closer inspection of the fishing boats, which were the largest of their kind Kemp had ever seen. He was full of admiration for the curve and sweep of their lines, the air that clung to them of warlike, swashbuckling audacity. Craddock, a repository of odd information, had assured him that these tunny boats were identical in shape, almost in size, with the galleys of the great fleet the Turks had thrown into action at Lepanto against Don John of Austria, when a sudden turn of the wind at the height of the conflict had lost them the battle, the war and the cause of Islam. Craddock had said, 'and the way the prow is drawn out to a point. That's where the iron bird's head used to be fixed. They could ram any other vessel of their day and cut it clean in half. But the wind changed. Otherwise, who knows? You and I might have been respected Hajji instead of what we are—'

Now it was the in-between season, but every year in spring and late autumn, the tunny-fishers took two great harvests from the sea, returning with their hands and faces painted with tunny's blood to divide up the catch according to the ancient equable principle of the Mediterranean, and to live in comfortable indolence for forty weeks out of the fifty-two. In this slack season they fished only at night, using the powerful acetylene lamps mounted on the boats to attract the fish to their nets. The captain was shocked by their amiable passiveness. 'They must work, sir,' he said, 'but you see they do not work. Soon we shall take these ignorant men into the army.'

'What are we going to do for fish, Captain, when that happens? That's the problem.'

'You see, sir, oil is buying everything. We will give our oil to Spain, Italy. Places that have no oil. They will send us fish. All these ignorant men must enter the service of our country. These men are dirty; they are not understanding hygiene. I would be sorry for you to see the kind of houses they are living in. In the army we shall teach them modernism. When you see these ignorant men again you will not know them.'

'That's something I'm quite certain about.'

Kemp rode back to the villa with the captain. They shook hands at the gate.

'Tomorrow,' said the captain, 'we will take all the mines away. Then an inspector will come to make his report to the ministry that all is safe. Next week we shall plant the palms. I do not like to swim, but I like to wind-surf. I will come here to wind-surf.'

'I'll be delighted to see you.'

The captain leaped on his Honda and departed, encircling the abandoned cement-mixer with a necklet of pink dust before roaring off into the muddle and haze of the morning horizon.

Kemp went back into the villa. He had been away hardly more than a half hour. The rooms were full of soft light filtered through closed shutters, and there were no sounds anywhere to suggest that Leila was up and about. He opened a shutter and found himself face to face with an Italian grandee painted in white tie and tails, all his orders on display on the balcony of a palace, and differing from any other man of great power and prestige in that he had allowed himself to be painted holding a bouquet of roses. For once the great man's eyes did not avoid his, but it seemed to Kemp that he detected the merest suggestion of a sardonic smile.

Chapter Twelve

Leila had locked herself in the bathroom, and came out when Kemp knocked on the door. There was a bleached, waxen look about her, the small triangle of her face turned by a single sleepless night into the face of a long-term prisoner who knew no more of the sun than the passage of brief reflections on high walls. Terror, inexplicable to Kemp, had de-sexed her. She placed her hands on his shoulders and reached up to touch his mouth with dry lips.

'Has the soldier gone?'

'He has. That was his motorbike you heard.'

'Why did he come here?'

'He wanted to show me over the beach. They're going to clean it up and make it into a bathing beach. They're all very proud of what's been done so far, and he wanted to get my reactions. Nothing more to it than that.'

'Will he be coming back?' she asked.

'Not so far as I know. He didn't say so.'

She went to the small square of window with a view of the beach and the sea and lifted a corner of the curtain. 'There are some soldiers down there.'

'They're lifting mines,' Kemp said.

'When will they go away?'

'Probably today. Or tomorrow.'

'I'll go and make coffee,' she said.

He followed her through into the kitchen. She poured the coffee and they sipped it. They could hear the soldiers chanting their choruses, which were of great sadness to a Western ear. 'I'm going to have to leave you for a few hours,' Kemp said.

'Must you?'

'It's something I can't get out of, much as I'd like to. A daily routine. I have to visit three or four ministries, pick up their handouts, and decide whether I can make use of anything they have to tell me. I come back here to put the copy together in the afternoon. By that I mean at two or thereabouts. You're nervous of the idea of being left alone, aren't you?'

She wrapped her dressing-gown more defensively around her body. 'I'm sorry, I can't help it.'

'You could come with me. I could take you to the Bab Medina and leave you there. You might feel happier to do that.'

'I want to stay here,' she said, as he knew she would. This land, for all its trappings of modernity, remained the Orient, and in some strange way the cultivated zest, the outward enthusiasm for all things new, only underlined the silent, stubborn conservatism of the past. The revolution had never wholly liberated womenfolk from a yearning for the yashmak and the veil. Kemp had accepted in advance that Leila would stay in the villa behind shuttered windows and barred doors.

'I'll make it earlier if I can,' he said. 'Would you like me to ring to see how things are going?'

'No,' she said, again predictably, 'I won't answer the phone.'

She went ahead of him to the door, insisting on peering through the little speak-easy hatch into the street, before taking off the chain. Suddenly the first storm of the year had funnelled up from nowhere. Kemp could hear the soldiers laughing and shouting with delight as they ran for shelter. Kemp kissed her hands and she slipped back quickly out of view. He stepped into the street. A frond torn from a palm sailed past like a ship in a boisterous sea, and heavy rain-drops were slapping on the grey flesh of prickly pears. She closed the door, and he heard her fix the chain. Then he made a dash for his car.

He made calls at the Ministry of Dams and Water Resources, the Ministry of Highways and Bridges, and the Ministry of

Tourism and Fairs, to sip coffee with officials of infinite courtesy and charm, the sons of desert horsemen dressed by Pierre Cardin in their environment of tension-control lighting, artificial zephyrs, and pocket computers.

'Mr Kemp, *marhaba*, and I know my day will be a blessed one when you are the first visitor to cross my threshold. Our esteemed friend Mr Salim made known to me your doubts about our trout-breeding project, and these I communicated to our Minister. He would be very happy if you could ring him at his office to make an appointment.'

'Mr Kemp, *ahlan wa sahlan*. The project report on the M1 desert highway has now been prepared for you. I do not know whether some foreign journal might be interested to print a few words—that would be very kind.'

'Mr Kemp, thank you, yes, I am well, *el hamdulillah* and I have quite recovered from the disappointment over the tomatoes. I have discussed the suggestion I made at our last meeting with my superiors, and they expressed great interest. I am sure you will be hearing from them. In the meanwhile your friend Mr Michael Jolly telephoned with a message. He wishes to see you urgently, and hopes you can meet him at the Eiffel Tower Restaurant at midday.'

Kemp took a cab to the Eiffel Tower, a fun-fair building profiled at night by electric lights like an enormous and garish toy version of the Parisian original in a glum environment of service stations and closed shops with dirty windows.

It was raining in earnest now, with roads turned to rivers and manhole covers popping out of the streets like champagne corks under the great, foaming upthrust of water trapped in the conduits. The restaurant was full of people, many of whom had gone there to get out of the rain. The service at the Eiffel Tower was extremely rapid, the prices reasonable, and the food good, but the great attraction was its decor. Every year in December the restaurant showed its respect for the customs of its largely Christian guests by putting up

Christmas decorations, a plastic Christmas tree sprayed with imitation snow, plastic mistletoe, stars of Bethlehem, shining baubles and bells, and they remained throughout the year until renewed in the following December.

Mike arrived, pulled off his wellingtons and hung up his sou'wester. They settled themselves at a table in the ante-room out of earshot of all but two aged men at prayer in a far corner, ordered *sharab,* the local soup, and the simplest of the many fruit concoctions on offer.

'Sorry to drag you out,' Mike said. 'About the only time I can get away. I'm holding the fort down the Fimisters' place, and I got a chum to come and take over for me while I was away. The Fimisters had squatter trouble last year. They made a fire of reproduction van Goghs to brew up tea on the bathroom floor.'

'You hear of it all the time. Anyway, nice to see you, Mike. Anything wrong then?'

'Something I thought you ought to know,' Mike said. 'It was all fixed up for me to take over at Dr Blanchard's when he went on leave, then suddenly he cancelled.'

'Had to put it off, has he?'

'No, he's not going after all. He's been kicked out. They've withdrawn his visa.'

'I can't believe it. Blanchard of all people. What on earth for?'

'The official reason given was a technical one. They said his qualifications did not comply with their requirements.'

'But he's been here for years. He's one of the best doctors in the country and they know it.'

'They can find a technical excuse for getting rid of anyone if they want to, and they wanted to get rid of him.'

'Has he stepped out of line in any way, then?'

'Yes, over you. As you know, he takes his job very seriously. He'd had a few when I went to see him and he told me all about it. He said he was convinced you'd been poisoned when he took you to the hospital, and he kept a sample of the stuff you brought up for analysis. This showed the presence of comium—a local form of hemlock they put in a drug you used

97

to be able to buy in the souk. Given in small doses, it's supposed to affect the willpower. Blanchard's theory was that the girl who worked for you slipped it into your curry.'

'But why should she, or anyone else, want to do a thing like that?' Kemp produced a half-hearted laugh.

'Because someone told her to, I imagine. Anyway Blanchard, being what he is, went straight to the Clinic, where they agreed that they *did* have vacant beds on the fatal night, and had no explanation for the fact that you should have been moved to the Oasis. His next stop was the Oasis, and naturally enough they stuck to the botulism diagnosis. When he threatened them with the Ministry of Health the Medical Superintendent told him he was impugning the national honour. Next day the blow fell.'

'And what do *you* think of all this? What do you think it's all about?'

'Blanchard's view is that you're the victim of a plot, and it may seem odd but I'm inclined to believe him.'

'Why on earth me? There wouldn't be any point.'

'There's more to come that may help to throw a light on things,' Mike said. 'You heard I called when you were out yesterday?'

'To pick up some keys you left behind, wasn't it? Did you find them all right?'

'Yes, I did. The girl I saw knew where to put her hands on them. She's very pleasant, isn't she?'

'That was Leila. Yes, she is very pleasant. I told her all about you.'

'We've been friends a long while,' Mike said. 'Five years is it? Can I be frank?'

'I should hope so,' Kemp assured him. 'What's on your mind?'

'Would Leila be a Libyan, as I assume by her name?'

'No, Lebanese, which is very different. She's a Libyan national.'

'Something about her face seemed familiar. I felt I'd seen it before somewhere, and then I remembered it was in one of Brian Fimister's magazines. You know he's president of the

Friends of Libya. He has a roomful of them. Handouts of all descriptions.'

Kemp experienced a kind of anxiety, studying Mike's smooth, unlined, untroubled face. Intuition warned him that whatever he was about to hear he would not enjoy.

'I spend a lot of the spare time that goes with my job trying to develop my memory,' Mike said. 'It's become a sort of hobby. They used her photograph in an article called "In Defence of Peace". I imagine she was the prettiest girl they could find. Would I be right in saying her second name is Miletta, and that she was a nurse at the Oasis?'

'Right,' Kemp said.

'The article was about the sacrifice made by Libyan women in the Uganda War. She was the wife of a heroic volunteer.'

'She told me about it. Her husband was killed.'

'Not killed,' Mike said, shaking his head sadly. 'Not according to this article. He was posted missing, which is a very different thing. Legally, he's alive. He could still be held prisoner in some African village at the back of beyond. A number of Libyans have. Or he could have been wounded and lost his memory. Unlikely though it may be, this man may still show up.'

The pit of Kemp's stomach fluttered, as if he had swallowed some tiny animal trapped in the soup. 'Nothing to stop you checking up,' Mike said, 'which you can do in a matter of minutes simply by phoning the Ministry of Defence. You could be in a very tricky situation, Ron.'

'It doesn't make sense,' Kemp said.

'On the contrary, that's just what it does. The thing about sitting around all day in other people's houses is that it gives you a lot of time to think,' Mike said. 'I've given quite a lot of thought to what's happened to you. My belief is there's a connection between that small dose of poison, the way you were shanghaied into the Oasis hospital where this girl was a nurse, and Blanchard being kicked out for asking questions. I'd say you've been set up for blackmail. Why isn't Leila at the hospital any more?'

'There was some trouble and she was suspended from duty.'

'So she took refuge with you.'

'At my invitation.'

'Of course. Who wouldn't invite a girl like that? This is a standard scenario, Ron. Having been on the fringe of the diplomatic scene I can tell you it's something that happens from time to time. More than one embassy person I know of has handed over secrets entrusted to them in return for the love of a beautiful woman.'

'I'm not a diplomat,' Kemp said. 'I have no access to secret documents, codes, lists of agents, or anything like that. In a word I have nothing to offer.'

'I think you'll find you have,' Mike said. 'Just what it is we don't know right now, but I'm sure we soon will.'

'Added to which,' Kemp said, 'if such a plot or conspiracy should exist, nothing would convince me that Leila would allow herself, consciously, to be mixed up in it.'

'Consciously is the word. She might still be used without having any idea of what was going on.'

The small cyclonic disturbance in Kemp's midriff had increased in intensity. Only an inner core of dismay stood firm in the disarray of his thoughts. He found himself tugging at his loosened collar while the owner of the place stood over them, palms spread in perplexity and self-reproach. 'He's worrying because you're not eating his food,' Mike said.

'It's fine. Tell him it's *kuwais*. I'm just not hungry. Not feeling myself. Sorry, this comes as a bit of a shock.'

'How long has Leila been in the house?'

'Two days. She moved in on Thursday.'

'You're incredibly lucky. Shall I tell you why nothing's happened to you so far? Because yesterday was Friday. They probably spent Thursday watching the place and questioning neighbours, and the next day was Friday. You know what happens. They go to the mosque and take their families out for picnics. Nothing's done. All the work gets put off until Saturday, which is today. Tonight is the night of the famous small-hours knock on the door. You have to remember this used to be religious crime. You had to be taken in adultery, biblical style, and the police took a mullah with them when they made the arrest. It still happens in places where they stone the girl. My God, Ron, lucky for you this isn't Saudi.'

'I suppose it is.'

'You have a few hours before the trap is sprung. Your problem is to get this girl out of your house as fast as you can and remove all traces of her presence. Could she go back to the hospital? *Would* she go?'

'She would if she could. I'm not sure that they'd take her.'

'No, of course not, why should they? If they did it would wreck the plan. Your alternative is to take her to the first hotel you can find with a free room. Escort her to the reception, shake her by the hand and get out. While the heat is on, you mustn't be alone with her. Whatever meetings take place while she's there have to be in the public rooms. I can tell you all this because I was in the legal section here, and we had plenty of headaches like this.'

'Whatever meetings take place,' Kemp repeated mechanically. His panic had gone, a brushwood fire quickly burned out to be followed by an exhausted listless calm.

He drove homewards through the water-logged streets under clouds being dragged away by a sharp-toothed breeze, and a final spattering of rain. Absolute gloom had been followed by numbed anti-climax. Viewed through the prism of this mood the incidents and adventures of the past days seemed coloured with folly. Youthful hopes and ardours re-encountered at his sedate age had proved boisterous travelling companions, urging him along too rugged a path. He was suddenly tired and full of bickering self-recrimination.

She let him in, and he listened to the door close carefully behind him and the rattle of the chain. Even the entrance-hall seemed to lie within the territory of the eavesdropper, so nothing was said until they reached the living room.

He took her hands. 'I'm truly sorry,' he said. 'The last thing I ever wanted to do was ask questions.'

'Go on,' she said. He could see that she knew what was

coming, and was resigned to it. 'Ask the questions. This couldn't last.'

'I just met a friend who told me more than I wanted to know. Why did you say your husband was dead?'

'He *is* dead.'

'He was officially posted as missing in action, and this means you're still married. You're not a widow, and you're obliged by the law here to conduct yourself as a married woman. If the true facts of the case hadn't come out today, they would have tomorrow, or the day after that. It was only a matter of time.'

'I've told you the true story. All the rest are legalities. I have proof of my husband's death.'

He was reproved by her dignity, but it had come between them. 'Is your proof acceptable to the law?' he asked.

'Two soldiers who were with him in the battle saw him killed. The body was left behind when they retreated. I could have taken them before the judge to ask leave to presume death. Two witnesses are enough. The judge would have accepted their evidence.'

'Why didn't you do that?'

'One of the men was sent to Chad.'

'It's months since the army came back from Chad. Where is he now?'

'Working as a farmer on a settlement near Tobruk.'

'So he could be found?'

She nodded, lips compressed.

She was slipping away from him, losing in some way tangibility. Like the maiden in the Celtic legend he only had to scold or chastize her, and he would lose her forever. 'Forgive me,' he pleaded, 'I don't want to drive you into a corner. I'm looking for some way out for both of us. Why did you never do anything to find this man who was in Chad? It's three years since your husband died in Uganda, and you're still officially married to him. Why?' He knew that there were questions that should not be posed and must not be answered, but there was nothing to be gained now by turning back, sensing as he did that the curtain must shortly fall on their brief comedy. Now the house will be empty again, he thought.

'If I'd have done anything legally it would have made it final.'

'But it was final. Your husband was dead.'

'I loved him. I prayed to God to raise him from the dead. If I'd have gone before the judge it would have meant that I'd abandoned him and denied God.'

'So in reality you didn't want to be free?'

'When I search my heart, no, I didn't.'

'You were the one who preached to me the necessity to forget.'

'Why remember pain if it can be forgotten?'

'You'd never go looking for that witness who's been farming in Tobruk, would you?'

She shook her head.

'So what's it to be now? Will you go back to the hospital?'

'If they want me back, yes. It's my life.'

'Something tells me they will want you back,' Kemp said. 'You're supposed to have been involved in a conspiracy that's clearly come unstuck. I was to have been blackmailed after being caught in bed with a married lady of Libyan nationality. Hence the food-poisoning or whatever it was I suffered from. Hence my stay in the Oasis Hospital, and the drugs frame-up they used to get you out of the place and, as planned, into my arms.'

'I would always be as honourable with my lover as with my husband,' she said, passing as she did do, he understood, finally beyond his reach.

'No one would convince me of anything to the contrary,' he said. 'The plot fell through because Arabs aren't very good at this kind of thing. Now, having mishandled the arrangements they'll probably accept defeat. Tomorrow or the next day you'll be hearing good news from Dr Ahmed. He'll apologize handsomely, ask you to come and see him and forget the past. It will suit you to say yes, but never trust him. For this man we're all pawns in a game. What the game is, we'll probably never know. Perhaps they weren't even sure themselves.'

Chapter Thirteen

The best solution, they decided, was that she should spend that night in a hotel, and see what the morrow brought forth. He took her to the Spanish place set in its own little wasteland on the town's outskirts, where the staff had shown themselves so helpful in the past. The tight-waisted, high-combed receptionist, who looked like a Sevillian dancer, seemed slightly surprised when he assured her that a single room was required on this occasion, but her welcoming smile was undiminished. The agreement was that he should come back on the evening of the next day.

Back home he set to work to remove the last vestige of her presence, a task abetted by the lurking atmosphere of the place, effortlessly re-asserting itself to restore the old anonymity. Within hours the walls had closed in on him; loneliness had moved in again like a deaf-mute lodger. A slow drip of water in the sink and the creak of a shutter were measured against the deep silence. He turned on the television for a glimpse of surgeons with their raised knives, before switching off again. The storm had brought down enough telephone lines to isolate him from the outside world. At about ten o'clock he gave up and went to bed.

He was awakened by his doorbell shortly before midnight. Kemp slipped on his dressing-gown and went down to answer it. He switched on the outside light, took off the chain, unbolted and opened the door. A man and a woman stood together haloed by the glow from his lamp against a starlit sky. Behind them one of the new police Toyotas crouched among the puddles. Kemp recognized the man, who was in a dark civilian suit, as the officer who had interviewed him at the customs. The woman, who was in uniform, he had never seen before.

'Good evening, Mr Kemp,' the man said. 'We are so sorry to be troubling you late in the evening. May we come in?'

'*Marhaba*,' Kemp said. 'Of course.' He led the way to the sitting room. 'You are welcome.'

'I am Inspector Aswad,' the man said, 'and this is Sergeant Khadra. Black and Green.' He smiled thinly as if he expected Kemp to be amused by the coincidence that both should have taken their names from colours. The sergeant in her blue uniform decked with polished leather equipment with pouches and straps, continued to show an uncompromising profile. She had the wide, staring eyes of a Queen of Egypt carved on an obelisk, and a nose continuing without interruption the slope of her forehead. Kemp knew that she had been brought along to cope with the possibility of a female prisoner.

'Mr Kemp, they are telling me that you are the sole tenant of this house,' the inspector said.

'I am the sole tenant.'

'There has also been information lodged that a person of the female sex is living here with you, contrary to the provisions of the laws for the enforcement of public morality.'

'That information is incorrect,' Kemp said. 'I'm quite alone. This you may verify for yourself.'

'Yes sir, we shall have to do that. Please excuse us for this intrusion on your privacy. We are under orders.'

'Of course. Would you care for me to show you round, or can I leave it to you?'

'We would prefer you to accompany us, sir, to observe our respect for your property.'

'I haven't any worries in that direction. Why don't you just go ahead, and take your time, while I relax with a cigarette.'

Aswad and the sergeant went upstairs. Kemp listened to the murmur of their voices and the soft thump of their footfalls overhead, as they went from room to room. They came down and he got up to meet them. The inspector marched towards him in a quicker-than-normal ceremonial fashion, halted and stood to attention. He bowed slightly in defeat, as if about to surrender a weapon. The sergeant stood at his back, arms pressed to her sides, and Kemp felt the basilisk eyes fixed on him like those of a snake-charmer keeping watch on a doubtful snake.

'Everything in order, I hope?' Kemp asked.

'Sir, everything is in order. The sergeant and I are wishing to extend our sincere apologies for this trouble. Our information was incorrect.'

'Well, never mind. Mistakes happen.'

The inspector's embarrassment remained evident. A study of his sensitive face reminded Kemp of the widely circulated story that a profound error in the young nation's vocational guidance programme had directed all those temperamentally equipped to be policemen into medicine, and all the nation's natural doctors into the police.

'If you wish, sir, you may make a formal complaint to the superintendent of our department.'

'I wouldn't dream of doing such a thing, Inspector. I'm quite happy to let the thing go. May I offer you a coffee?'

'*Shukran*, Mr Kemp. It is kind of you. At any other time.'

Kemp would have liked to persuade them to stay; to have helped him to banish even an hour of the night.

'Nothing at all? Are you sure?'

'The sergeant and I are responding warmly to your hospitality, but you will please excuse, as we are prevented by duty.'

'Well, I'm sorry you won't have anything, but I quite understand.' They shook hands at the door, the inspector bowed again, and the sergeant turned on him a last glance of her enormous, indifferent eyes. A moment later he heard the car start up, the splash of its tyres through the mud, and the brief falsetto howl of the desert dog, disturbed in the building site across the road. Kemp went back to bed.

At seven in the morning Mike Jolly rang. 'Did anything happen last night?'

'It all went as you predicted,' Kemp said.

'You don't mean you had visitors?'

'I do indeed.'

'No problems, though?'

'None whatever. I was ready for them. They took it quite well.'

'The Fimisters got in last night, and I'm back in the Compound,' Mike said. 'Come over and have breakfast.'

Kemp drove down the coast road to the Compound, where the joggers were already in action, watched by Arab early risers in their cars, who had come there in the spirit of Westerners putting themselves to some inconvenience to watch an incomprehensible tribal dance.

Mike awaited with fried eggs and smuggled bacon in a company room identical to the last detail, including the speckle-throated carnivorous plant, to the one up the road in which Kemp's meeting with Wendy Winters had taken place.

'So it was the old two a.m. knock on the door as foreseen?' Mike said.

'Midnight to be exact. A very smartly turned-out plain clothes inspector, and some sort of power-hungry police woman. Both polite, many apologies for troubling me, but they were under orders, etcetera.'

'But they found nothing.'

'Not so much as a smudge of lipstick on a cup.'

'Where's Leila now?'

'I took her to the Spanish hotel.'

'What an escape. Think of it, you could have been wading into a plateful of black beans in a cell in the model prison at this very moment. How did Leila react? Was she upset?'

'No way of saying. It was all a lot calmer than I expected. I hate to think it, but it may even have come as a bit of a relief. I mean the idea of moving out. She's been under a lot of strain.'

'You're still convinced she wasn't in the know—?'

'More than ever. She was scared stiff of being caught with me. There's no budging her from her story that her husband was killed in action. Two soldiers who were with him saw it happen, she says, but she never bothered to establish legal proof of death.'

'And you believe that?'

'Yes I do.'

'Well, I believe he's dead too,' Mike said. 'They don't take prisoners in that kind of war, and the hyenas take care of the wounded. It's this legal proof thing that bothers me. Why didn't she do anything about it?'

'She's still in love with him,' Kemp said. 'A matter of sentiment.'

'I suppose that's about it. So what are the plans from now on?'

'Nothing really. I suppose things will go on much as before. I'm very grateful to you, Mike, for all this.'

'What's happening about Leila?'

'A hundred to one she'll go back to the hospital. We'll probably see each other once in a while. I hope so. She's a very nice girl.'

Mike smiled in his tolerant way. 'I know you'll see her once in a while. Why shouldn't you? As long as you keep it within reason.' He shook his head. 'It's been a funny business, hasn't it? Very mysterious.'

Craddock lived only five semi-detached company houses away. In a desperate attempt to combat the monotony of the surroundings he had changed the position of every piece of furniture he had found it on taking over, hung a calendar advertising baby food over the simulated coal fire, and banished the inevitable plant to the lavatory. These efforts only seemed to Kemp to have underlined the impression of standardization.

'No ill effects of any kind, I hope?' Craddock asked.

'Never felt better,' Kemp told him. 'I enjoyed the rest.'

'Better stay away from stuff out of tins in future.'

'Or unvetted curry,' Kemp said.

'I expect you've come about the booze,' Craddock said.

'The party's on Saturday. When can I pick it up?'

'I'll give the Scotsman a ring,' Craddock said. He went into the next room, leaving the door only slightly ajar, and Kemp heard the low rumble of his end of a conversation on the phone. A moment later he was back. 'We can go down there in an hour's time if you like. I'd better take you. No street name and no numbers as usual. I was quite forgetting it was fixed for Saturday. Like me to give you a hand?'

'Mike will be there pitching in, but come along by all means if you feel like it. We'll find you plenty to do.'

'Want me to pass out the usual maps, marking the check-points with alternative routes?' Craddock asked.

'If you like, but it shouldn't be necessary. I'm not giving the kind of party where we have to worry about the police. Flash is out. We'll have the Black and White, and anybody who doesn't want that can drink Mike's Bio-Malt beer of which we'll have several gallons. I'm going to see to it that this is a good party, not a shambles.'

'You're wise,' Craddock said. 'Very wise.'

'They have three addicts at the General Hospital with partial blindness. Naturally the powers that be are cracking down.'

'The small-time operators are to blame,' Craddock said, 'but I agree with you. Stick to the real thing, whatever you have to pay, and you can't go wrong.'

'I made it clear I didn't want any fancy-dress nonsense,' Kemp said.

'It won't make any difference. Half of them will turn up in something weird and wonderful whatever you say. What's the objection?'

'The objection is that it brings down heat,' Kemp said. 'They picked up Bill Lavers at a road-block last week on his way to the Broadbents' party. He was going as a flasher with a basketwork donger under his raincoat. They held him at Gargarish for twenty-four hours for a psychiatrist's report. The Arabs simply don't understand this kind of thing.'

'Trouble is a lot of your guests are coming all the way from the rigs. Bill Chambers for one. He's stuck down in Sidi Hocine. This is Wendy and Bill's moment to be seen together in public again. Big occasion for them.'

'I hope they'll have a good time.'

'It's quiet down on the rigs,' Craddock said. 'I've been

down there. Turns them into escapists. They want to escape into a world of fantasy. It's to be expected.'

'As long as they keep their fantasies out of my villa,' Kemp said. 'I've got too much to lose.'

Magnus Thirkettle, who was the intermediary on this occasion for the distribution of whisky smuggled in by an Australian pilot employed by the government, also distilled what was regarded as reliable flash. He had made money by inventing a species of mechanical tyrannosaurus which rolled down any road, snatched up wrecked cars, crushed and compressed them in its jaws, then trundled away to dump the concentrated remains, reduced to a few cubic feet, onto the nearest wasteland. Thirkettle's machine eventually cleared the streets, it was estimated, of a thousand wrecks, enabling him to set up in business as a booze baron on the royalties he earned. He was in competition with less scrupulous operators whose customers were often taken ill with such symptoms as loss of memory, speechlessness and temporary paralysis, or were apt to behave in a wild or illogical fashion, convincing many of the Arabs among whom they lived that the West was now hopelessly decadent, and its collapse only a matter of time.

The location of the small distillery in which Thirkettle's five stills turned out hundreds of bottles of firewater a day was kept a close secret. He received Kemp and Craddock in his villa in a bulldozed no-man's-land known to the expatriates as Knightsbridge—a soft-voiced, unworldly looking Orcadian belonging to a religious sect noted for their fanatical observance of the Sabbath, who served them tea with digestive biscuits, put on a Bach cantata tape and discussed prices with a dreamy aloofness that seemed to disinfect the transaction. Thirkettle mentioned that he had recently bought the biggest farm on his native island, and that one day, when he retired, he would go back there to breed a rare variety of sheep, of which only sixteen examples had survived.

He was in the make-believe as well as the liquor business. Flash straight from the still, colourless and flavourless in plain unlabelled bottles, cost £12, but this was unacceptable for party occasions, so most people paid £2 extra for the same flash to which colouring and a Japanese chemical flavouring had been added, and which was supplied in a whisky bottle bearing a brand name. Labels of all kinds were produced in Malta for this purpose. Bottles of recognizable shapes such as 'Dimple' Haig and Glenfiddich were in great demand, being brought back empty, with some inconvenience, by expatriates from their UK trips, and flash in such prestigious disguise fetched £20. Thirkettle was quite happy to display his wares— which he did with quiet pride—and to discuss these matters. He refilled their cups with Earl Grey, excused himself, then came back with the case of Black and White.

Kemp picked out a bottle and examined the seal over the cap. 'Any objection to my trying this?' he asked.

Thirkettle shrugged his shoulders. He looked hurt. However he reached down a small glass, opened the bottle, and poured enough whisky into the glass to cover its bottom. Craddock reached out and took it, sniffed, and nodded approvingly. He passed the glass to Kemp who took a sip.

'All right?' Craddock asked with a trace of impatience.

'All right,' Kemp said. There was no doubt that the whisky with its smooth, delicate flavour was genuine.

'Magnus and I have been doing business together for quite a few years,' Craddock said. 'I don't think you'll find much wrong with anything you buy here.'

Kemp unloaded the whisky at his villa, dropped Craddock off, then drove over to the Spanish hotel. This time a receptionist he had not seen before was on duty, and her manner was indifferent, almost to the point of hostility. There was no reply from Leila's room, she said, but Kemp insisted she was there. Eventually the lift door slid open and Leila came into view. Kemp went to meet her, instantly detecting a composure and a serenity about her that spoke their own message.

He took her hands and they moved out of range of the receptionist's dejected inspection. A few hotel residents, all of them elderly men and quite motionless, were seated at random throughout the lounge like chess pieces left on a board by players who had gone away after an uninspiring game. 'Did you talk to the hospital?' he asked, certain in advance what her answer would be.

Two shallow depressions under her cheekbones had filled up since the night before, and tender little muscles at the corners of her lips were ready to launch their smiles.

'Yes, and it was exactly as you said it would be.'

'They want you back?'

'I'm starting again tomorrow. They've been trying to get in touch with me. The investigation's over and Nurse Martínez and I have been completely exonerated. The Management Committee has written to us.'

'And you spoke to Dr Ahmed?'

'He asked to be put on the line, and he couldn't have been pleasanter. He said he felt a sense of personal victory that we'd been vindicated.'

'The sense of personal victory is a nice touch,' Kemp said. The moment had come to tell her of the night's happenings, but he sensed that they would have shrunk in importance when viewed from the pinnacle of security regained. 'The police came last night,' he said. She showed no sign of alarm, nor did he expect her to.

'They arrived as I thought they might. Very civilized. Most apologetic. Went through all the rooms, downstairs and upstairs, opened all the cupboards, probably looked under the beds. Nothing. They went away again.'

'What was said? Did they tell you what it was all about?'

'Nothing more than the usual police formula. Information had been received regarding an alleged breach of the morality laws, etcetera.'

'So nothing came out about who was supposed to be involved?'

'Not a word. It's all right. You weren't mentioned by name. Whatever they were after, they didn't get it. I think it's safe to say that you can forget about that particular episode, and take up life as before.'

'I'll never be able to do that.'

'Of course you will. Why shouldn't you?'

'I'm human,' she said. 'When anything like this happens to you you're never quite the same again.'

'We had a little time together and a little love. Your work is your life. Go back to it and think about things. Let's give time a chance. The door isn't closed. I can't solve your personal problems for you, but we can always discuss them again whenever you want to. You have only to pick up the phone.'

Driving away, Kemp isolated a feeling at the back of his consciousness that took him by surprise. It was one—he could hardly admit it to himself—of relief. This short-lived affair, presented to himself—as all its predecessors had been— as an emotional watershed, had brought in its train a kind of exhaustion. Love, as he knew, was an exhausting business, becoming more so with every year that passed, to carry him further from the suppleness and spiritual resilience of youth. Once again, inevitably, an affair of the heart had plunged him back into the strain and the turmoil of adolescence, and now fatigue, masquerading as better judgment, was about to come to his rescue, to restore him gratefully to its own brand of maturity.

As soon as he turned the key in his door and opened it, the sudden clamour of the telephone in this embalmed silence startled him. He picked up the receiver.

'Is that you, Ronald?'

'Kemp speaking.'

'Tried to get you several times. The morning's always the best time to get through.'

The voice was at first wholly alien, then terribly familiar. 'Who's that?' Kemp asked.

'This is Jimmy Jimson. How are you faring? Well, I trust. I'm ringing because it's on the cards I'll be in your part of the world at the beginning of next week, and I thought it would be very nice if we could meet up.'

'Next week? Well, I suppose we could, I expect to be in town.'

'I've been held up over the visa, but it should come through any day. There's a deal in the offing involving the purchase of oil and it occurred to me that it was high time we should meet again to see if we could get that little scrap-iron venture of ours off the ground.'

Kemp caught the false affability in the voice. He could see the smile moving like a crafty animal under the beard. Once again he recognized the telephone's ability to isolate certain truths of personality sometimes obscured in a normal face-to-face encounter.

One international telephone call in three, Kemp remembered, was monitored. Awareness of this fact sharpened his thinking processes. 'The scrap-iron venture? Oh, yes. Well, I'm not altogether sure about that.'

'I didn't expect much enthusiasm at this stage, but I think you'll change your mind when you hear what's suggested. At all events we can have a chat about it. Nothing to be lost by that, eh?'

No harm in stalling him, in seeing the man again, and listening to whatever he had to say. Kemp would not have gone out of his way for another meeting, and nothing would have induced him to make a second trip to Malta. Tripoli was a different matter. Jimson would never be allowed in if he were regarded as a suspect person, and if an oil deal with the government was afoot there was no better or more respectable motive for him to be there. Kemp was half-hoping, at the encounter to come, to listen to some new, totally impossible proposition that could be turned down out of hand, and then dismissed from mind without the slightest aftermath of regret.

'We couldn't have picked a better moment, the market's at an all-time high,' Jimson said.

'That's good news.'

'At this stage I don't think there's any more to be said. So we'll leave it at that, then, and I'll call you as soon as I get in. Bye for now.'

Chapter Fourteen

'Do you really expect me to put these things on?' Kemp asked Craddock.

'Nobody's forcing you to do anything,' Craddock said, 'but does it really matter? What does it cost to humour them? It's the gesture that counts. Nothing to stop you nipping away as soon as the thing gets off the ground, and changing back into what you're wearing now. I'll probably do the same.'

Craddock wore a shirt made from a Union Jack under jungle fatigues, a German Army helmet, death's head emblems on each sleeve and a chain and padlock round his neck. Kemp suddenly burst out laughing. 'You look absurd,' he said.

'That's just what's intended.'

'Where do you find this stuff?' Kemp asked. He picked up the black leather jacket, examining its detail almost in disbelief. It was decorated with a pattern of steel balls radiating from a central Iron Cross. A large swastika had been sewn on the red pullover worn under this. The shiny plastic trousers were provided with a belt from which dangled a pair of handcuffs.

'From the fancy dress pool,' Craddock said. 'Military gear is in great demand, and I had to take what I could get. If you'd have made up your mind a day or two earlier it would have helped.'

'And most of them will be dressed up in this sort of thing.'

'You can be sure of that. They love it.'

Kemp began to change. 'Is this a punk party?'

'It's anything. They don't know the difference. These are adult men and women trying to be kids, trying to be something else. Punks, skinheads, hippies, Mohicans, new

116

romantics—what do they know or care? They try to look as crazy as they can. It helps them to let their hair down. They need it, poor sods, after six months in hell-holes like Sidi Hocine.'

A car horn sounded in the street and the desert dogs awoke all round to set up a howl. 'That's the first of them,' Craddock said. They clattered down the staircase together, Kemp alarmed to think what his hobnail boots would do to the marble floors. Mike, in charge of the drinks, placed himself behind a trestle table charged with the whisky and beer just inside the door. He was dressed in rockabilly style, with bleached jeans and black jackboots with white laces. Kemp had been astounded that he should have agreed, seemingly with alacrity, to dye his hair black for this occasion, and then he had understood. Mike inhabited his own kind of desert, and this was an escape for him too. Mike's friend Ivor, in charge of the music, had been issued with tapes by the Stones, Buck's Fizz, Abba, with instructions backed by dire sanctions to keep the volume down. Guests were to be hit with slugs of whisky as soon as they came through the door, but after that Mike was to serve watered-down drinks. All windows were to be kept closed. About one party in five was raided by the police these days, and Kemp explained to Craddock that this was inevitably through the lack of reasonable precautions. In case of a raid there was a normal drill by which the police's entry was delayed by demanding to see and to be allowed to read their warrant, while the liquor was flushed down the toilet, but Kemp was quite sure that such an emergency would not arise at the well-organized party he was determined that this should be.

The first guest came through the door—one of a contingent that had driven the 800 miles from Tibesti, largely over desert tracks, in under two days. Kemp who had just started back in horror after catching sight of himself in a mirror, was amazed to find that Harry, whose shoulders he clasped, should show not the slightest sign of surprise. For his part Kemp found Harry hardly recognizable for the right half of a stubbly beard, evidently grown for the occasion, had been shaved away together with the half-moustache, leaving an unbalanced smile proclaiming both embarrassment and bravado on the clean-shaven side of his face. Dodging into view from behind Harry was his wife Alice, all parts of her uncovered skin encrusted with white paint, with a large safety pin through the lobe of each ear, and another apparently through the septum of her nose.

'Harry, Alice, wonderful to see you. Absolutely wonderful. What's it to be? A shot of the hard stuff by courtesy of the Leader's personal pilot, or Mike's weak beer? Grab yourself a jar. Straight or with Bengashir water? Ice? Glad you could make it. Really happy. Must be on your knees after that trip.' Kemp was surprised at himself. Eight hundred miles to a party—how could they do it? And how did they manage to get through the roadblocks?

Harry put down his glass. 'Well, I really needed that. Know something, that's my first glass of the real thing for six months.'

'Let me top you up,' Kemp said. 'Mike, we need another bottle. Alice, Harry—here's to you and the fellow prisoners sweating their guts out back in Tibesti. Cheers, eh? This won't do you any harm.'

Five more oilmen and their mates crowded into Kemp's field of vision. He saw Indian patterning in blues and reds on a woman's forehead, a plastic Mohican crest cemented to a scalp, and perfectly simulated tribal scars on a cheek. Among this group there were technicians and scientists, serious men, some of them having subjected themselves to long and arduous and soul-draining disciplines to get where they were in their profession. Now they were in the mood to relax and play the fool. More guests crowded through the door, and Craddock at Mike's side was helping with the drinks. Kemp, who had put down his glass, raised it to his lips again, noticing as he did so a strangely anaesthetic odour. He sipped cautiously, then drew Mike aside. 'Would you taste that?' he said.

Mike tasted. 'What do you think of it?'

'I don't know. What is it?'

'Flash, I would have said. I must have picked up the wrong glass. How did flash find its way in here?'

'Somebody must have brought it.'

'Why should they bring flash, when they know I serve whisky?'

'Search me.'

Three bottles of Black and White were open. Kemp poured a little whisky from each of them and sniffed at it. 'This is okay,' he told Mike, 'but the other's flash. It would explode if you put a match to it. The question is where it came from, and where the rest of it is?'

It was at this point that he noticed a change in the atmosphere, in the noise level, in the feel of the party. Someone had slipped under Ivor's guard and put on a tape of Pigbag, roaring pop funk. Couples were beginning to dance in a desperate fashion. Drinks were put down and kicked over, and Kemp, listening to the sound of feet crashing through broken glass, the thump and wail of the music instantly turned up again, and the howls of the desert dogs that not even the closed windows could shut out, was reminded of the massacre of his neighbours' religious peace.

He cantered round the rooms, one after another, testing the odour of abandoned glasses, immersing a fingertip in the liquid some of them contained and licking it. In some cases he suspected the presence of flash, or of flash cut with whisky. Now he wondered whether, confused by so much sniffing and sampling, his imagination had taken over. Renewing the ties of old friendships, he had clinked glasses many times, but there were minor warning sensations unlike those he associated with straightforward alcohol—weightlessness, then a feeling as though a tiny caterpillar was exploring the surface of his cheek. 'Humphrey, whisky satisfactory in every way?' 'First rate, dear boy, absolutely first rate.' 'Clive, notice anything about the whisky?' 'I'm too far gone to notice anything, ha, ha. I'm sure it's very good.' 'Wilfred, there you are. Tell me, I'm a little worried about the booze—' 'Well now you mention it, I was wondering myself.'

A man whose name Kemp had forgotten found them, joky

but concerned. 'Marvellous party, Ron.' He held out his hands. 'Look at my fingers. Funny, they've gone numb.'

Kemp went back to Mike and Craddock. Mike had had all he could hold, but Craddock was remarkably sober. 'I want to look at those bottles again,' Kemp said. 'Half of them are gone,' Craddock told him. 'Our friends have been walking off with them and setting up little parties of their own. Why, anything wrong?'

'I don't understand what's happened. This party is going like all the others. They're demented. Just listen to that row.'

Craddock shrugged his shoulders, coolly smiling, ironic and indifferent. He took off the helmet he was wearing and put it on Kemp's head. 'My advice to you, Ronald, is to relax. They're having a good time. Only live once.'

The fastidious Ivor came to tell him that the music was out of control. He had other bad news. 'They've put on a video cassette about cannibalism and sex. I locked the door at the top of the stairs but some of them forced it and went up on the roof. They're copulating and being sick all over the place. Someone fell off the roof and hurt his back. They're trying to get an ambulance. Whatever they've been drinking has set fire to their brains.'

'They've been drinking flash,' Kemp said.

'The lights are on in all the houses down the road. I'd better tell you—there's a couple in your bath. Some of the women are auctioning off their pants. I think that one who painted her face white has gone mad. She keeps trying to stand on her head.'

Where had the flash come from? How had it got there? Kemp continually asked himself. 'We've got to get rid of them somehow or other,' he said.

'They'll never go,' Ivor told him.

'No, they won't. Not on their feet.'

The Sex Pistols had routed the rest now, shouted down even the dogs. The villa shook like a storm-buffeted ship, and a resonance of brash guitars had set all the loose-fitting metal windows awhine. Flash went with the uniform he was still wearing. It made supermen of them for five minutes, and then turned them into underdogs ready to howl together in united misery. *God save the Queen and the fascist regime*. Kemp snatched off his helmet and threw it as far as he could across the room, just as there was a tug at his sleeve. He turned to find Harry there, eyes watering and his half-beard flecked with foam. 'Wendy wants to talk to you, Ron.'

'Wendy?'

'Wendy Winters. She's in the kitchen.'

Kemp pushed through the dancers and the sprawled bodies and went to the kitchen, where he found Wendy propped against the sink into which she had been trying to be sick.

'So you made it, Wendy. But why are you on your own, and for Christ's sake, why are you crying? Where's Bill? Didn't he come?'

'No.'

'But why didn't he? I invited him. I invited you both. Who does he think he is?'

'We're finished.'

'I don't understand you.'

'I let him down.'

'All that's past history. You got together again didn't you?'

'I went back on the booze. He turned straight round and took off for Sidi Hocine. This is the end of everything. It's all over.'

'It's not all over. Nothing's ever all over unless you want it to be. Listen, Wendy, I'm going to see Bill. I'll go down to Sidi Hocine myself if I have to. You and Bill are made for each other. All you need to do is to get away from this place. It's living out here that's killing you.'

She was holding a tumbler which a falling tear had just missed. He took it from her hand and threw the contents through the window.

'Where did you get that stuff?'

'One of your friends gave it to me at the door.'

'Oh my God,' Kemp said. 'I've got to do something. They're poisoning everybody. Wait here for me, will you? I'll be straight back.'

'Don't hurry,' she said. 'I'll be all right. Where do you go to through that door?'

'Into a garden full of gear-boxes and old tyres.'

'I need fresh air.'

'I do too. Wait for me, and I'll come with you. There's a beach just across the wall, and not all the mines have been cleared. We'll go for a walk together.'

Mike intercepted him, swaying a little, a hand held over his left eye to restore single vision. 'A raghead wants to talk to you, Ron.'

'A raghead—don't give me a heart attack. You're joking.'

'He said he was a friend of yours and you'd invited him. Go and see for yourself.'

Kemp shoved his way through to the entrance hall where he found Salim awaiting him, dressed for the first time in Kemp's experience in a goat-hair cloak in old-fashioned local style, conferring on him both dignity and aloofness—patrician Goth in a scene of Rome in decay. The sight was an instantly sobering one.

'Good evening, Salim.'

'Good evening, Ronald. You invited me to your party, and here I am.'

'*Marhaba*. My house is yours. It's a privilege to welcome you.' Kemp held out his hand and spoke as one sane man to another in a world of fools. 'Please forgive my ridiculous appearance. This is a fancy-dress party, and I'm obliged by the rules of hospitality to keep up with the rest.'

'This I quite understand. We have heard all about European fancy-dress parties. It is interesting for me to be present, and to see one for myself.'

'Let's get away from the noise and find a quiet place for a chat,' Kemp said. He steered Salim by a circuitous route to the ruin of a conservatory at the rear of the villa, where a single indestructible cactus had survived to attest to the long-departed Italian presence.

'I must confess my visit was not only in response to your invitation, but to the laws of friendship,' Salim said. 'When you spoke to me of your desire to give a housewarming party, my reply to you was that I might telephone your neighbours, explain to them what was intended, telling them at the same time that you were regarded by my department as a good friend, and asking for their indulgence.'

'I remember that.'

'I did this, but I confess now that it may have been a mistake. It drew official attention to what you were intending to do. This party was something that everyone knew about.'

'I've let you down, Salim. I know you did what you could for me. Something very strange has happened here. I have a feeling that I've been double-crossed. My intention was to organize a quiet celebration. As you see, they've turned my villa into a madhouse.'

'You may have enemies you do not know of, Ronald. Our town is full of spies and those who double-cross. There was a man sitting by your door as I came in. I know of him but I do not like him. All his money comes from the sale of illicit liquor.'

'What's going to happen, Salim? I can see my reputation with your people is at stake. What should I do?'

'I have little influence, but the little I have I have tried to use. People here have been breaking the law. They have been drinking alcohol. They have appeared unclothed in full view of your neighbours upon the roof. Wild music was being played and there was much shouting from windows. A call has been made for an ambulance to take away an injured man. People who have telephoned to protest have been received with abusive words. They have said to them such words as fuck-off, which are hurtful to their religious feelings. I'm sorry, in our law you the host are responsible for all these things.'

'I can't explain to you what it's all about, Salim, because I don't know myself, but I'm sure it's all part of a conspiracy. Somebody is out to get me.'

'This I believe, too. As I said there must be a secret enemy. But now I must tell you what is to happen. The police have agreed not to enter your villa. A roadblock has been set up at your entrance to the main road. They have a list of all your guests.'

'How on earth can they have got hold of that?'

'That I cannot tell you, but I know that all your guests will be stopped for questioning when they leave. They must tidy themselves, and go as quickly and quietly as they can. They cannot escape the police, who will speak to them all and ask for samples of their blood. You must say to them to co-operate. They must not argue, or disagree with the police, or call them bad names. In this way no anger will be caused.'

'No chance of their being hauled straight off to the lock-up, let's hope? Or even God forbid, Gargarish?'

'Certainly not Gargarish, any more. If I put on your fancy dress I will be treated as an insane person, but for foreigners now this is okay. What we must do is to finish this party quickly and tell all the people to go to their homes.'

'After that, what?'

'Tomorrow you may come to my office. We will go together to talk with a friend, who has a little more influence than I have. Perhaps he will agree to speak with the Minister in your favour.'

They stood up to clasp each other's shoulders. A sort of stagnant calm had suddenly spread through the villa as if the revellers behind the thin partition wall had been brushed by the finger of extra-sensory perception in their drugged state, and warning shadows had fallen upon them. The dancing was at an end. Small whimpering noises reached Kemp of weariness and protest. Somebody twiddled at a radio dial and a quartet of voices plucked from the depths of the ether chanted nasally and with infinite resignation.

'Now I think I will go,' Salim said. They turned to make for the door when summer lightning flickered behind the dust of the whole wide expanse of conservatory glass, a single huge pulse-beat thumped at the soles of their feet through the floor, and several hundred panes rattled in their warped frames. 'Oh my God,' Kemp said, knowing that in that instant the worst thing that could possibly have happened had happened.

Chapter Fifteen

Many people and countless animals had come to a sudden end in the minefields sown to guard the beaches all along the coast, small unreported calamities having become so commonplace that special apparatus had been devised to remove human or animal remains with minimum risk to salvage teams thus employed. Such apparatus, kept in readiness at principal fire-stations, resembled a gigantic pair of sugar tongs, to be used in conjunction with a hook on an extensible pole, and within ten minutes of the explosion the firemen were on the scene, picking their way towards the small white bundle among the marram and sea-pinks discovered by the searchlight fixed to their tender.

Wendy's body was expertly drawn by the hook into a position where the tongs could be used, and within a matter of seconds lifted onto a stretcher to be carried to the ambulance following the fire-engine. Despite their familiarity with tragedy and the self-discipline with which they had learned to face horror, the ambulancemen were unable to repress their disgust at the incontinence provoked by the few seconds of Wendy's conscious agony, and washed themselves scrupulously before setting off for the morgue.

The members of the party at Kemp's villa were left in no doubt as to what had happened for, within seconds of the explosion, three rings Wendy had taken from her fingers were found with a suicide note and an empty glass on the worktop of Kemp's kitchen. Several of the guests, taking fright, had run out of the house, jumped into their cars and tried to make their escape, only to fall into the hands of the police at the roadblock. Five minutes later Inspector Aswad and his men burst into the villa to place all who remained under arrest.

Aswad's manner was composed to the point of detachment. He was a religious man imbued with the fatalistic heresies that had grown up round the core of his faith and a sneaking belief that evil as well as good came from God. When, therefore, he said to Kemp, slumped in a chair staring at the ground, 'You sir, are responsible for these severe crimes,' he was devoid of anger, being unable wholly to absolve God from some small share in this criminal responsibility.

Kemp, stunned, trapped in a grotesque dislocation of justice, feeling the sense of abandonment and betrayal of a young child accused of a misdeed he does not even recognize as such, could find little to say. One of Aswad's subordinates gestured to him to stand, for as a man under accusation of a major crime he was subject to a protocol designed to abase the insolent and frustrate the potential suicide. His shoe-laces and his belt were taken from him, obliging him to keep his hands in his pockets to hold his trousers up. The men that pushed and pulled at him, snapping their commands in an incomprehensible patois, did so with a kind of squeamishness they might have shown in contacts with the corpses of those who had died of a contagious disease.

'*Quel shay, quel shay.*' 'Say something.' He was expected at this point to make a statement, a routine declaration of innocence, and the man who had taken his belt from him, holding it between the tips of his fingers, was ready with his notebook. Kemp, his nose and eyes suddenly beginning to run, could only shake his head.

From the corner of his eye he saw Harry, furious as a Brahmin in an untouchable's embrace, being held by one Red Crescent medical assistant while a second plunged a hypodermic needle into his arm. A doctor checked pulse rates and a nurse, nose wrinkled in disdain, went round spraying the room and its contents, both human and inanimate. As a sop to the *shari'a*—the religious resistance that still demanded its pound of flesh—the oilmen's wives, squealing their protests, had been veiled as adulteresses before being led away.

Despite an infatuation with progress and modernity,

certain other concessions existed to a mentality that had not wholly freed itself from the barbarous past, one being the vestige of an ancient law of the desert that held a man accountable for the offences of all those he had sheltered in his tent, reinforced in its time by a prospectus of floggings and minor amputations. Aswad came back to this again. 'I ask you to listen to me, sir. You must listen to what I am telling you. You, sir, must accept the punishment for everything that has happened in this house.'

Italian colonialism had bequeathed a severity by which a man apprehended for a serious crime was forthwith put in chains, on the grounds that the prospect of being thrown into a black hole in the ground to be kept there for the rest of his life was likely to goad him into desperate action. The men who had taken away his shoelaces and belt now produced fetters. Shackles were first snapped over Kemp's wrists and ankles and the chains attached to these.

At this moment the young doctor who had done with the last of the guests now being led away by the police, hurried across full of tongue-clicking concern. *'Istanna ... istanna.'* He wagged a reproachful finger in the policemen's faces, ordering them in a wrathful torrent of Arabic to remove the leg irons. He then squatted in his pin-stripe suit as comfortably as any vegetable seller in the market to examine Kemp's ankles. His bag was fetched and he found lint and sticking plaster to cushion the bony protuberance on which the weight of the irons would lie. The policemen looked on respectfully while this was being done, then the irons were snapped back.

The doctor warned Kemp earnestly. 'Not to allow sores to form while the skin remains unhabituated. Beware of ulcers in these places.'

His warning jerked Kemp out of the lethargy into which he had fallen. He raised his arms and listened to a rippling series of clanks. When he let them fall two loops of chain crashed down to form symmetrical coils at his feet, and he realised that he would have great difficulty in walking.

'When are they going to take these off?' he asked the doctor.

The doctor was full of sympathy. 'I do not know the habitudes of prisons. Perhaps after a week, perhaps after a month, they will remove them. I am sorry. This is something I cannot say.'

Chapter Sixteen

The doctor had had no time to familiarize himself with the procedures of the Centre for Social Readjustment to which Kemp was taken. It had only been operational for a month. Chains were out here, and prison officers dressed like karate instructors swooped on him instantly to remove them, and handed them back to the policeman who had brought him. Dazed and demoralized as he was, Kemp responded more to the stage-scenery than the details of this experience. The Centre's reception office might have been that of one of the oilmen's clinics—themselves under the spell of the austere romanticism of the new airport and the National Bank. The overriding impression was of the pursuit of emptiness, of deep silences momentarily broken by gabblings in foreign tongues, of air lifeless, neutered with a perfumed disinfectant. This place imposed a new brand of isolation. It offered nothing to engage eyes or mind, apart from brief human encounters that fell short of being contacts, such as the view of the young lady seen through the glass shutters of a facsimile bank counter who listened to Kemp's details croaked through a microphone, punched them on a card, and fed them into a computer.

A medical examination was inevitable. Kemp was led straight from the bank counter into what might have been a manager's office in the same idiom: a room constructed of glass blocks, and a monosyllabic Arab with the high-domed forehead and grey goatee of Sigmund Freud. 'Sit, stand, bend, straighten, mouth open, close, breathe deeply, cough,' the doctor said, prowling round him, spotlight shining from his forehead, like an illicit hunter who had discovered an animal in a trap. The next stop was a cubicle where Kemp surrendered the black leather jacket, plastic trousers and hobnail boots, and was given in exchange a suit of blue, coolie-style pyjamas. After that he was taken to his cell.

The Centre had been adapted from an Italian architect's prize-winning design for a car factory in Turin, where the problem had been to isolate top management from the distraction of noise of any kind as well as visual stimuli likely to impede the creative process. The Arabs, seeing its potentialities, had leaped on it with delight, and Kemp's cell—allowing for the removal of everything that might suggest luxury or even comfort—was almost a replica of the room designed for the managing director. It was in effect a metal-lined sphere with a circular platform constituting the floor. The furniture—bed, chair, table and television set—were of rigorous simplicity, all matched in battleship grey to the anodized aluminium of the walls. A copy of the Koran lay beside a military-style telephone on the table, and a correctly oriented prayer-mat was fixed to the floor. A sliding door closed off a cubicle containing an Arab-style latrine, and a faucet and bowl for ritual ablutions. There was no window, but a circle of fluorescent tubing high up in the curve of the ceiling spread a halo of cold twilight. A wall-notice over the bed, lettered in the plainest of Arabic script, said, '*Peace on you, and welcome O traveller on the path of regeneration.*'

Kemp lowered himself to the bed. He closed his eyes and instantly, as though the supports to his consciousness had been snatched away, he was gone, down, and back, and beyond, and afar, resisting airborne voices that summoned him, even the far-off jingling of alarm bells which finally transformed itself to a telephone ringing incessantly in his ear.

He awakened uncomprehendingly and seconds passed before, eyes half opened, he identified and located the sound and groped for the receiver. 'This is your Block Counsellor.' The voice spoke to him from Central Europe, at once sharp but indulgent. 'You're a heavy sleeper, my friend, so this morning our first private chat will be cut short. Please I would like you to answer very rapidly and truthfully to my questions. It is important to tell me what first comes into your head. My first question is, what do you wish to do most at this moment?'

'Go back to sleep.'

'You will allow me please to rephrase this. You wish to evade responsibility. To bury your head in the sand.'

'I'm tired. That's all I can say.'

'You have problems we shall explore together. First, I must ask you to explain the reason why you were wearing a garment bearing on it a swastika when you were admitted to the Centre.'

'A swastika? I'd forgotten. Yes, I was. And you're asking me to tell you the reason? There wasn't one. It was a joke.'

The man on the line barked his derision. 'No one will wear a swastika for a *joke*. This is in response to parental domination. Were you dominated by your father or your mother?'

'By neither as far as I know.'

'You did not respond consciously to that domination but I can assure you it was present. This symbol of violence offers a threat to those who seek to assume the role of a dominant parent. I wish to share with you your guilt.'

'If I felt any to share, I'd share it,' Kemp said.

'You have caused a woman's death. It is impossible not to feel guilt, however determined you are to transform this response into something you can accept. Everything for you, my friend, is a fiction, everything is a device to avoid reality. You dress yourself in the uniform of a hangman, you tell me for a funny joke. This you believe yourself, but you must not ask me to believe it. You are tricking other people but the joke you are playing is on yourself. You are like a man who compels himself to follow the profession of a miner because he wishes to re-enter his mother's womb.'

'I have caused no one's death. The woman committed suicide as the result of a broken love affair.'

'We shall carry out a deeper explanation of the subject of self-delusion when we talk next, tomorrow. We shall have many more talks and you will see that I am very patient. I promise you that in a week from now you will be ready to accept your guilt. Then you will be on the road to self-knowledge and rehabilitation. This is enough for today. Tomorrow we shall speak again.'

Kemp put down the receiver. He lay back on the bed and fell into a light doze. A small clatter alerted him and a tray slid into view through a flap that had opened like a mouth in the wall by his bed. It held a bowl of black beans, a glass of tea, and a curled object like a boot-sole he recognized as unleavened bread.

He drank the tea, then fell back on his bed, trying with no real hope of success to sleep again, but now the full aching awareness of his predicament could no longer be held at bay. Kemp remembered with acute detail stories he had once brushed aside of the grim adventures of other Europeans held in prison on serious charges such as currency offences and espionage. They had been spirited away to disappear from sight for weeks and months, and even when finally located by the embassy people, consular access had been denied. They had suffered what he was suffering now, the special agony of the Western man, severed as if by a stroke of the executioner's sword from the routines of his daily existence.

Kemp pulled himself to his feet and went to the latrine. The door, electric-eye operated, slid open with a hint of a sigh, then closed behind him. Ceramic foot-prints indicated the correct position of the feet. He urinated, took a pace to the rear, and water—mysteriously flushed—swirled then disappeared in the aperture of the tiled floor.

They had taken his watch, and glancing down as a matter of habit at the pale disc it had left on his sun-reddened skin, he knew how complete was his involvement with time; how firmly the rhythms of his body and mind were yoked to the hours. He picked up the telephone in the hope that the Block Counsellor might answer, since talk on any level and with anybody would have been welcome at that moment. The line was dead. In the moment of replacing the receiver he detected an electrical purr, the sound of a loudspeaker being switched on overhead, although there was no sign of one in the featureless curvature of the ceiling.

Now a pulsating high-pitched wail began, a remote spatial

wheedling that suddenly came close, filled his head with its appeal, then faltered into silence. It was the midday call to prayer. He felt relief. Time had not wholly forsaken him.

Hardly had the sound died away when a glass bull's eye glowed over the cell door, which slid back, and Mike was there. He crossed the threshold a little dubiously, as if treading on ice. A web of thin shadow projected by the lighting clung to him, extinguishing his eyes and remodelling his nose into a predatory hook that belied the mildness of his character.

Kemp reached for his hand like a man overboard about to be pulled from the waves. They sat on the bed and Mike's head rotated slowly in an apprehensive survey of their surroundings. 'Daunting scene, isn't it? I've heard quite a bit about this place.' He leaned across to sniff at the beans. 'They give you kebab on Fridays,' he said. 'Anyway, how are you?'

'Don't ask me. I can't get my thoughts together.'

'I can imagine that. They interrogate you? Rough you up in any way?'

'No. What happened to the others?'

'They hauled us all off to the station, kept us a couple of hours then let us go. Naturally this is only the beginning of it. This could be the night of the long knives. Apart from Wendy, Croker broke his back.'

'Oh my God. Did you see Wendy?'

'Yes, I saw her, and it was instantaneous. Thank heavens for that. I think it's something you have to try to put out of your mind. There was nothing going for her any more. She was finished. If it's possible to say such a thing, you might even decide it was for the best.'

'I wish I could take that point of view, but I can't. There must have been some sort of way out.'

'Pointless to talk about it. Unfortunately what's happened is going to damage the community. It's given the mullahs the excuse they were looking for to declare war on decadent Westerners.'

'Do they count for all that much?'

'If they howl loud enough the government will do

133

something about it. They don't like foreigners even if they need them. This gives them the chance to clear out the ones they can do without. Half of us are going to lose our visas.'

'Myself included, I imagine.'

'You've got more than a visa problem, Ron. I hate to tell you, but they're really out for your blood. The police, anyway.'

'I know they're holding me responsible for the lot ... tell me Mike, what really happened last night? Where did the flash come from? Did Craddock have anything to do with it? Bad flash is half the price of good whisky.'

'I wouldn't put it past Craddock to have switched the drinks, but if he did I doubt if the few extra pounds to be made would have bothered him. You told me you thought you might have been set up over that nurse who moved in with you. What I've just remembered is that that Filipino girl who worked for you used to work for Craddock. Craddock could be taking orders from someone. It's a wild sort of idea, but I suppose it's possible. You told me you suspected a plot against you that fell through. Perhaps this trouble at the villa is the second instalment. The second string to the bow if you like. What makes me suspect something of the kind is that after they let us go I was taken on a hush-hush visit to see someone in the Defence Ministry. That's why I'm here.'

The electrical purr started again and a woman's voice broke in on them. It was dreamily persuasive but persistent, like a television commercial in praise of a brand of chocolate. '*Buon giorno. Oggi andiamo a considerare il cómpito del invididuo di fronte alla Società*...' Mike shook his head. He grinned wearily. 'Italian,' he said. 'Must have got their tapes mixed.'

'*Siamo cittadini di un mondo morale*...'

'Non-associational confinement, black beans and moral uplift,' Mike said. 'I'm told they copied the system from Korea of all places. Anyway, it's an ill wind—this place is certain to be bugged but there's not much chance of their hearing what we're talking about with the row going on.' Mike shifted closer to Kemp on the bed. He lowered his mouth to Kemp's ear. 'The main reason I'm here is to tell you

you have to get out of this place as fast as you can. There's only one way of doing it.'

'What's that?'

'Try for bail—'

'*Lo stato lavora per tutti per costruire . . .*' The voice above their heads was raised in an ecstasy of admiration of the state's efforts on the people's behalf. There was an intake of breath, a pause for dramatic effect. Mike waited for the speaker to launch into her argument again.

'What's the chance of getting bail?'

'It sounded good.'

'Could there be some sort of a deal at the back of this, by the time they took you round to the Defence Ministry?'

'I got the impression of something like that. The man I saw seemed to be putting out a feeler. They're not in a position to offer you a straight deal, as I understand it, because you come under the Ministry of Justice. Hence the bail idea, which I suspect is your only hope. In about a week's time you'll be given a preliminary hearing at which it's ten to one you'll be sent for trial before a people's court. You know what that means.'

'I've attended a couple of trials.'

Then I don't have to tell you. Naturally you could wait up to two years before your trial came up. In the meanwhile you'd be here. Two years of black beans and moral suasion.'

'Don't you see the Embassy doing anything?'

'Not on past form. This is the most advanced penal institution in Africa,' Mike said. 'The screws call you brother. Nobody's going to shine a light in your eyes and ask you questions. But two years. Think of it.'

'I don't want to.'

'And I'm not talking of the sentence. Twelve years is the average. That's what they slapped on Moriarty for the big currency fiddle.'

'I'd hang myself with my braces.'

'You'd never get the chance to. There's not even a cord in those pyjama pants you're wearing. They'd see to it you came to no harm.'

Kemp stared down at the palms of his hands. Suddenly sweat had appeared in the creases. He could only remember panicking once before in his life.

'The feeling I had was that basically they had nothing against you. Not at the Defence Ministry anyway. The way the man was talking he made it sound like a nice friendly game of chess. My impression was that if you came to an arrangement with them, they'd stick to it.'

'But what sort of arrangement? That's what defeats me. What are they after?'

'I wasn't given the slightest hint of that.'

The assault in Italian, alternatively honeyed and severe, appeared to be slackening in emphasis and pace. Mike hurried to bring to a conclusion what was left to say. 'I was more or less told that someone would be coming to see you today. Whatever they offer you maybe you should take it and think yourself lucky.'

'Even if I got bail, how would I get out of the country?'

'Get out of here first, then worry about that.'

' . . . e adesso, caro fratello vi lascio per il momento. Tanti auguri . . .'

'She's finishing and I'm going,' Mike said. He got up.

'Come and see me again. As soon as you can, eh Mike?'

'Sure I will. Soon as I can make it.'

'You'll let them know at the Embassy—'

'For what it's worth. I'm going over there now.'

They walked to the door together, which slid open as if operated by an electrical device able to reach the mind.

A guard waited in the even dimmer light of the passage beyond. Mike turned to wave and was gone.

After a long banishment, time came into its own again following the evening call to prayer, after which the television switched itself on to provide a resentful commentary on world news, and an instalment of yet another serial about English hospital life.

Dr Ahmed arrived late in the day. He walked towards Kemp, moving a little stiffly as he always did, as if on excellently fitting and well-managed artificial legs. At half-distance from the door he stopped with his arms at his side to bow, his mouth raised uncertainly at the corners in a smile tinctured, it seemed to Kemp, with embarrassment and apology. The desert, simplest of all environments, had never encouraged these people, Kemp mused, to develop a style of their own, and now they were ready to take the impression of any mould. He was sure that Dr Ahmed had visited Japan, and been impressed by all that he had seen there.

'Good evening, Mr Kemp. I hope I am not disturbing you. I seem to be getting into a habit of paying social calls at rather late hours.'

'Good evening, doctor. *Marhaba*. I can't imagine that anything would disturb me in my present situation. Please take this chair and I'll sit on the bed.'

Kemp's attention was distracted for a moment by a familiar rattle. The wall-flap opened and two cups of tea on a tray slid into sight. 'Will you join me? The tea here is excellent.' He handed a cup to the doctor who nodded appreciation, took a ritual sip and put the cup down.

'This visit must come as a surprise,' Dr Ahmed said. 'I'm sure I am the last person you expect to see in these circumstances?'

'Not at all, doctor. I was warned that someone might be coming here to discuss matters which are obviously of great importance to me. I had an intuitive feeling that that person would be you. Somewhat late in the day I'm beginning to see you as the key figure in my life's story in these past few weeks.'

'You have been putting two and two together.'

'I think so. Yes. I've been very obtuse.'

'Was any indication given you as to the purpose of this visit?'

'There was. Is this something to be discussed when the chances are that someone is taping down everything that passes between us?'

'That could not happen.'

'I'm glad to hear it. I wish I felt so confident.'

'No one could do such a thing without my authorization.'

'Well, I suppose I have to accept that. You seem to be a powerful man as well as a determined one, doctor. I have an idea that you'll stop at very little to get what you want.'

'Please allow me to explain that this is something that is forced upon me. It gives me no cause for satisfaction. By nature I prefer persuasion and sincerity. You will remember that at the time of our original meeting I did all I could to enlist your sympathies, but was unsuccessful. It was a matter of vital necessity to have this co-operation.'

'I wish you could have spelt out to me what was likely to happen to me if it wasn't forthcoming,' Kemp said.

'Believe me, I am sincere in telling you that I am unhappy you should find yourself in your present difficulties, particularly by the charge of criminal responsibility in a fatality. What you would call manslaughter.'

'There is no country in the world where they would call what happened last night manslaughter.'

'There I have to disagree. You furnished the alcohol causing this woman to do what she did. Had you not done this she would be alive now.'

'I had nothing to do with her death. She came to my party determined to do away with herself. She was a well-known alcoholic who'd just served a sentence in one of your prisons for drunkenness, and she was drunk when she arrived.'

'These are allegations which you will be given the opportunity to argue and to prove at the trial.'

'I have an unpleasant feeling,' Kemp said, 'that her death is to be made to serve your purpose, whatever it is.'

'You would have been charged with other grave offences,' Dr Ahmed assured him. 'The death was something nobody foresaw. It has strengthened the case against you. No more than that.'

'And strengthened your hand in a deal I'm told you've come here to propose.'

'That is so, possibly. But by chance.'

'A chance you will take advantage of?'

'I am bound to. The issues can be so great that they take control of a situation. There are some occasions when immoral actions become moral.'

The wincing embarrassment was there again. In this country and this city salvation called five times a day from the high places, and it was hard to shut its message out of the ears. The formula it offered was a simple one, but there was nothing of comfort in it for the secret policeman, the conspirator, the assassin or the spy. These Arabs, Kemp thought, took what the Chinese, the Japanese and the rest of them had to offer, but with many a regretful glance back at their virtuous desert identity. 'Doctor,' Kemp said, 'surely we don't have to go on a truffle hunt after morals. You do what for one reason or another you're bound to do, and I do the same. We bow to force majeure. Forgive me but let's forget about our consciences. The only thing that concerns me is getting out of this place as fast as I can. If that's something you're here to talk about, let's get down to it with no holds barred.'

'It might be possible, as you will have learned, to arrange a deal. It would be in return for services rendered.'

There was something in his manner that suggested to Kemp the loss of face of a normally well-conducted citizen detected by a railway inspector in a paltry swindle over a ticket.

'All deals are, aren't they?' Kemp said.

'Having come to an arrangement with you, you would be released on bail.'

'When?'

'Forthwith.'

'Does this mean I'd be free to come and go as I pleased?'

'Relatively free, let us say. An agent would be assigned to you, to safeguard our own interests, but he would be inconspicuous. It would not be permissible for you to contact any person, or to use the telephone unless the agent was present. The young man I have in mind is a pleasant fellow and has attended an English University. You would not find his company irksome.'

'And then what?'

'You would carry out your side of the bargain to our satisfaction.'

'And having done that?'

'The person charged with keeping you under his care might prove lax in his duties.'

'That still leaves me in the country, presumably on the run, and therefore almost certain to be picked up again.'

'I do not promise you an exit visa and a first-class seat on a plane, but a way will be found. A way will be found.'

'I see. And what am I expected to do?'

'Something extremely simple. First of all, let me say we know of your contacts with Vickers and Jimson, and what is at the back of them. We have a monitoring system that extends beyond the frontiers of this country. It is as effective in Malta, which you recently visited, as it is here. The devices we employ are the most—' he groped for a word.

'Sophisticated,' Kemp suggested.

'Exactly. Sophisticated.'

'You obviously know of my contacts with Vickers when I've been sending him a news story on average once a month ever since I've been here. I deal with him because he's a first-class agent. Jimson is a different matter. I've met him once only and I know nothing about him. I listened to what he had to say, and no more than that.'

'I share your pleasure in the charm of the Barraka Gardens,' Ahmed said. 'Jimson is well known to us. He is a man without loyalties. Vickers had fallen under his spell. To employ the usual expression, he had been recruited.'

'We've been friends for years. I find it hard to believe he'd lend himself to trickery where I'm concerned.'

'Soon you will discover what sort of a friend Vickers is to you. You will learn for yourself the truth. Then you will decide. You have all three been kept under the closest surveillance, and we've been able to discover the exact nature of the proposition put to you. You refused at first to allow yourself to be involved in any way. That was all to the good, because it increased your credibility. Do you understand what was at the bottom of these overtures?'

'I didn't even want to think about it. Something I wanted to put out of my mind. Why should anyone offer me a lot of money for nothing? How many attempts have there been on the Colonel's life to date? Five, is it? I suppose this was to be another one. They were looking for a safe beach.'

'You could tell them where to find one.'

'I suspect that you made sure I could. This must go back to that story I sent to *Le Monde*,' Kemp said. 'It was the only newspaper that wanted to use it. They put it in on a day when there was no news.'

'It served its purpose almost better than hoped for. We expect Jimson to arrive in this country tomorrow. Although you rejected his first proposition out of hand, it appeared to him later that you were wavering, and he will be coming, as he has told your good friend Vickers, in the hope of persuading you to change your mind. You are the first person he will wish to contact, and when you leave here you will go back to your villa and wait for him to call.'

'I have an idea of what's coming,' Kemp said, 'and I should warn you that I am a bad actor.'

'That is all to the good. Jimson is too intelligent a man to be tricked by acting of any kind. The meeting will call for no use of the imagination. You will invite him to the villa for a discussion, where he is bound to put to you a number of questions to which you will reply in a simple, straightforward and truthful manner. Show him the beach and tell him all he wishes to know, just as if he were some visiting tourist. No more than that. Remember that if anything occurs to arouse Jimson's suspicions and he takes fright, bail must be cancelled. Should this happen I should be unable to be of further help.'

'And should everything go off to your satisfaction?'

'Today is the 31st of the month. The agent will be obliged to remain with you until the 7th. On that day he could fall asleep while on duty, permitting you to walk out of the house, or perhaps lose sight of you while strolling together in a crowd. These are small matters of detail, and of little concern to us. Be sure that something along those lines will happen. You can rely upon me.'

Take whatever you're offered, Mike had urged. Mike believed that the Libyans would stick to any deal they made, and Kemp believed that too.

For a moment Kemp had been tempted to ask, 'what guarantees am I being given?' He changed his mind. How could there be any guarantee? He was in the man's hands. Moreover, he had already summed Ahmed up as a sensitive man, troubled by twinges of conscience, and concerned with self-justification and face, and he had no desire to tip the balance of what he suspected to be a benevolent neutrality by calling his word into account.

'What can I say, doctor? I have to agree.'

Dr Ahmed nodded. 'Good,' he said. He was watching Kemp's face closely. 'Mr Kemp, I am curious. Why have you chosen to spend so many years in Muslim countries?'

'I'm a creature of habit, doctor. I knew what to expect of Arabs—anyway, I thought I did. In the end I suppose I felt at home.'

Ahmed shook his head, as if in sorrow. 'I have learned something concerning your grandfather, who was in Mahir. I would have wished to know this before.'

'I thought he'd long been forgotten,' Kemp said.

'Not by the Arabs. He was a great man.'

'I never knew him. I understand his life ended in failure. By that I mean in the public sense. His career came to an abrupt end. He saw himself as a success. He was a happy man.'

'Ahmed held out his hand. 'Mr Kemp, I hope we may meet again in pleasanter circumstances.'

Chapter Seventeen

They were on the roof of the villa, sipping Jimson's smuggled-in whisky, and looking down over a spread of foreshore and sea.

'Well, to get down to the nitty gritty,' Jimson said. 'I brought traveller's cheques because they seem to be the most convenient vehicle for lolly these days.'

He eased forward in his chair to reach his hip pocket from which he extracted a small black folder embossed with a gold crest. 'This slim little wallet contains forty cheques each for one thousand Swiss francs.' Kemp found that Jimson had captured his hand, clasping his fingers over the wallet when he took it in a manner that he found in some way distasteful. '*Avec nos compliments et remerciements*,' he said. 'As of yesterday the Swiss franc stood at three eight five. If my arithmetic is correct you're getting a little better than ten thou out of this which, as I understand it, should solve all your most pressing problems. I hope you'll agree that Agence Presse Libre have been pretty open-handed. One thing I'll say for them, they're not cheese-parers.'

'They're not. That I have to admit.'

'Happy then?'

'Quite.'

'May I make a suggestion?' Jimson asked.

'Please do.'

'I don't know whether you're thinking of carrying all that loot around with you, otherwise it might be an idea to post the cheques back home, one at a time, to some *personne de confiance*. Just a thought.'

'Not a bad idea. I might well do that.'

Jimson's smile moved under his beard, gathering together

tight little creases below his eyes. He exuded satisfaction. 'You know, Ronald, now that everything's settled and we're home and dry, I must tell you I was somewhat nonplussed at all that resistance you put up to what seemed to me a very simple and effortless transaction. It's something I wouldn't imagine you'd have given a second thought to.'

'It was the size of the figure involved that made me feel jittery,' Kemp said. 'If it had been a hundred or so I might have felt different. I'm not used to these vast sums of money.'

Jimson laughed his mock exasperation. 'Oh, my God, now he tells me. Still, never mind. A deal's a deal. Okay then, let's have it. Where's the famous beach?'

'Here.'

'What do you mean, here?'

'Down there. Two hundred and fifty yards of it. Roughly from that ruined tower over on the right to the fishermen pulling up the boat.'

'Is this some sort of a joke?'

'Why should it be? This is *the* beach. It's safe. It's been cleared.'

'How can you be so sure about that?'

'I'll tell you,' Kemp said. The agreement with Dr Ahmed had been that he should tell the truth. Was it enough that he should do that and no more? Could not the slightest hint be dropped of the dangers the truth concealed? He shied away from the question he had posed himself. An over-sensitive conscience in this kind of dilemma was something no man in his right mind could afford. To hell with Jimson and his friends. 'Notice those goats between here and the water's edge?'

'Yes, nice animals, aren't they? Good condition.'

'To their owners they're highly valuable property. They're tethered on twenty or thirty yards of line apiece and there's not a blade of grass or anything down there of an edible nature they can't reach. The owners turned up with them yesterday as soon as the word got round. There was a bit of a scuffle over the grazing rights.'

'You're very observant. Something I'd never have noticed.

Goats getting down to business with nice fresh grass.' Ignoring the tundra of rubbish spread by the army engineers in the foreground, his eye ranged affectionately over the scene. 'Idyllic, isn't it? Kind of thing Claude would have painted. Where every prospect pleases, eh? So they took up the mines and let in the goats. What do you suppose made them do a thing like that? Do you really go for that line about building up tourism?'

'It's not the whole story. There's no doubt they're going to need tourism when the oil runs out, but they're going to phase out minefields in any case.'

'Why should they do that?'

'Because they're to be replaced with prefabricated forts.'

'Prefabricated forts? That's a new one. Where are they buying them?'

'Israel.'

'I don't believe it.'

'Via Central America. When you're in the arms business the last thing you do is worry about where the hardware eventually ends up. The first of them is due to be off-loaded next week. They take twenty-four hours to put up, and can't be knocked out by any conventional weapon.'

'What are those big boats out there, the other side of the tower?'

'Tunny-fishing boats. This is the off season for tunny. They fish with lights for whatever they can catch.'

'Why lights?'

'They attract the fish. They go out about ten or fifteen miles as soon as it's dark, and put down their nets.'

'*Every* night?'

'Weather permitting—which it usually does at this time of the year. They don't catch much, but they're always there.'

'What time do they get back?'

'About dawn, or just before.'

'Always?'

'Inevitably. It's the way all Mediterranean fishing goes.'

'That's interesting,' Jimson said. 'I'd like to see them at their work. Singular boats, aren't they? Can you see there'd be any objection to my taking a snap of them?'

'Why should there be? Take as many as you like. It's quite a poetic sight on a clear night to see them fishing all along the horizon.'

'I'm sure it is. Kind of thing that has great appeal for me. Do you paint, Ronald? Something I've always wanted to do. I find inspiration in this kind of spot. Anyway, let's go down there and take a look round, and take a few snaps of the boats.'

Leading the way down the stairs Kemp felt the void, the newly-scrubbed and disinfected lifelessness of the villa rise up to engulf him like a fog. They went out onto the beach by the door through which Wendy had stumbled to her end, and set out along the track towards the sea. Kemp assumed Dr Ahmed's agent would be keeping a perfunctory watch on them through the slats in the venetian blind over the bedroom window. He was a friendly and enthusiastic young man, a collector of Beatles records and a connoisseur of London railway stations who had lived delightedly in mean streets behind Euston and Kings Cross during his student years in England, from which—to his huge regret—his political activities had eventually procured his banishment.

'Where are the minefields?' Jimson asked.

'The nearest one is about a hundred yards away on our left. It's marked out with tapes. You can't see them from here.'

'I can see where they've dug out mines and put fresh turf back.'

'They laid them in patterns of semi-circles like the floor tiles you see in Italian farmhouses,' Kemp explained. 'There was no possible way of walking through them in a straight line without getting yourself blown up.'

'No place for a beachcomber, eh?' Jimson uttered his rich chuckle.

'It remains a bit of a mess as you see. What I hope they'll do is clean it up and leave it as it was, and not throw thousands away tarting it up.'

'They have oil. Why should they worry? Any idea what sort of mines they use?'

'Not the faintest.'

'I thought you might. They seem to tell you so many things. You find some very ingenious pieces of mechanism in that line these days.' Jimson warmed to the subject. 'The latest operates by a magic eye,' he said with relish. 'It can be set for any proximity you choose.'

'No end to progress, is there?'

They reached the nearest boat. Fishermen squatted at the edge of its shadow to mend their nets while others nearby brewed tea, or slept. Jimson waved and one of the fishermen got up to offer a fish. 'Marvellous boats,' Jimson said. 'Date back quite a few years, I imagine. They *made* boats in those days.' He took out an Instamatic camera to photograph the boat from several angles, and the fishermen, who were both superstitious and shy, covered their faces.

Jimson took a few more general shots of their surroundings, of the old tower, of Kemp's villa, and a clump of wilted palms sprouting through miscellaneous jetsam that remained to be cleared. Then, having come to the end of the film, he slipped out the cassette, wrapped it in silver foil, and dropped it into his pocket.

'Any reason why we shouldn't have a swim round?' he asked.

'Bit on the cool side for me,' Kemp said, 'but nothing to stop *you*. Want to go back for a swimsuit?'

'What's wrong with underpants? I don't see anything but goats around.'

'I'll change my mind and join you,' Kemp said. They undressed and waded into the water, which was colder than Kemp had expected. He submerged his body with a quick, ritual plunge then splashed back to the shore. Jimson, fifty yards out, was swimming strongly. He dived a couple of times then headed back. Two turbaned fishermen were watching them from one of the big boats. None of the fishermen could swim a stroke, and they were filled with admiration for those who could.

Jimson came out of the sea laughing, the sunshine glinting everywhere in small watery pockets in his skin. He pulled up his clinging underpants to conceal the trail of dense black hair descending from his navel and squeezed the last of the water out of his beard. 'Bit nippy, eh?' he said. 'Sun's still warm. Warmer than Malta.'

'You can look forward to a good month after the first rains. I expect I'll be down here most days.'

'I envy you, Ron, I really do. This is a nice beach. I'm crazy about water sports of all kinds. Ever done any spear-fishing?'

'Not with any success. I can't clear my ears.'

'I mention spearfishing because you learn to judge the fishing prospects before going into the water. I could have told you what I'd find out there before going for a swim. The underwater profile matches the beach. You have a smooth bottom with a very gradual slope into deep water, and no dangerous rocks. No currents to worry about either. Wonderful for children. You're going to have a great time with this beach. Don't forget to invite me down next time I'm over.'

'At this stage am I allowed to know what's happening?'

'My dear Ron—a thousand to one, nothing. I know you won't believe me but I haven't the faintest idea what this is all about. Surely I told you before? The people I work for hoard information like a squirrel hoards nuts. They hope it will come in useful one day. This time they want to know about a beach in Tripoli, next time it's the depth of the metalled surface of a strategic road in Brazil. I'm not kidding. Believe it or not, I'm quoting an actual case. What in hell's the good of stuff like that to anyone? Don't ask me. You and I know there's not the remotest chance they're ever going to use it, but they insist on having it. And what interests you and me is they're prepared to pay good money for it. So why, I ask, should we worry, Ronald? We deliver the goods, and we pocket our cheques. The labourer is worthy of his hire.'

Strolling back, they were close to the villa now. A woman in something like a purple nightgown squatted to milk a goat, an old man, wonderfully balanced, lay asleep on the narrow top of the garden wall, and two small children were stoning a cat. The scene embodied all the elements of the deepest Islamic peace. 'Tell me something, Ronald,' Jimson said. 'I'm curious. What made you change your mind about this business? You seemed so deeply distrustful in Malta. Considering the glowing reference I know Teddy Vickers gave me, I felt a trifle hurt.'

'I suppose I was taken by surprise. As you pointed out at the time, I was in the information business just as Vickers and you were. The thing was I'd always traded at the bottom end of the market, and I hadn't the faintest idea what the going rates were at the top.'

They both laughed. Jimson said, 'Listen, it's on the cards I may be staying over tomorrow. If I do could I possibly pop over again for a quick dip?'

'Whenever you like,' Kemp said. 'I'll be working here all day. Come over any time. Make it lunch if you can. Should be a nice day again. The forecast is good for the next week.'

'That's very gracious of you,' Jimson said. 'Very kind. If I can't make it tomorrow, would the next day be any good?'

'Any day you like,' Kemp said. 'Be glad to see you.'

Jimson was at the Bab el Medina hotel within twenty minutes. He threw his clothes into a suitcase, settled his bill and was out in ten minutes more. He told the driver to take him to the airport, arrived thirty minutes before an Air Malta plane he had not intended to catch was due to take off, and hustled his way through customs and passport control just in time for the final call. An hour and a half later he was in Malta, where he phoned Cairo from the airport.

'Lucky as ever, James,' Brandsteller said. 'I was just going out the door. How did the trip go?'

'Better than expected,' Jimson said. 'But the way things are shaping we're going to be very short on time.'

'We're short on time anyway. Pharaoh won't budge on the dates. It has to be the sixth or it's all off. We've been running round in small circles.'

'I hit on a fantastic thing here,' Jimson said. 'One of those pure flukes. The other problems are okay, but this is a bonus.

Listen, do they still make those phoney dhows for rich men to fool around in up at the old dhow yard at Bahra?'

'I would assume so,' Brandsteller said. 'I imagine it's about all the business they do these days. You mean a lateen-sail ship for the spice trade with a sauna and gold-plated bathroom taps? Sure they do.'

'What I have in mind is a sambuk.'

'Forty-five feet and a hundred tons maximum,' Brandsteller said. 'Carvel-built. The best ones used to come from Ma'ala, near Aden.'

'That's it.'

'Well, you might find one out at Bahra. You'd better grab a plane and come over here, and we can go out there and see. I'll find out what I can while you're on your way.'

Five hours later Jimson was seated beside Brandsteller at the wheel of his Pontiac as they rumbled northwards up the straight, flat road from Cairo, leading through the muddy and labyrinthine town of El Rashid to the coast.

'So how do matters stand?' Jimson asked.

'Ibrahim Hawi is all set in Tripoli,' Brandsteller said. 'We had a signal from him.'

'What sort of a boat are you sending?'

'You know those launches used on the cigarette-smuggling run from Tunis to Naples? Like one of them, but three times the size. We had it built with an exceptionally low profile to get round Parsons' objections.'

'But a radar problem still exists?'

'In a minimal form. It's bound to. We depend to some extent on speed.'

'What I propose solves all these difficulties,' Jimson said. 'When I saw all these boats down there on that beach, I said to myself, why not? I knew it was the answer. We'll have the photographs of them tomorrow. I'm convinced we could fix up a sambuk to match one on the radar screen. Can you see anything against it?'

'Yes, the time factor. Today is the first, and the action is on the sixth.'

'And nothing can be done to get Pharaoh to change his

mind?'

'We're up against a brick wall. He's still adamant about the mullah who told him it was his good luck day, in addition to which it's the anniversary of the Suez Canal crossing in the Yom Kippur war. He's staging a big parade. What we're doing is all part of the package. This is the kind of act the Caesars used to put on in ancient Rome.'

'Is he the nut-case they say he is?' Jimson asked.

'Put it this way, he lives in a world of his own. Parsons took me along to the Palace the other day to give him a sit-rep on the plan. "I shall vanquish the Libyans," he says. "I shall drive them into the deserts, just as my ancestors did." "Which ancestors was that, Mr President?" Parsons asks him, our impression based on what he always tries to tell you being that this guy's family came from poverty a generation back. "Rameses III," he says. He was talking about something that happened in about 1200 BC.'

Jimson shook his head. 'How much did you say you've handed over so far to keep him alive?'

'Officially 25 million,' Brandsteller said. 'It's probably a lot more.'

'And he won't even wear a bullet-proof vest?'

'He says it wouldn't be manly. When a crowd forms,' Brandsteller said, 'they all start to grab at his hand. Naturally his bodyguards move in to knock them about a bit. "Go away," he tells them. "I am with my children." What can you do about a guy like that?'

'I'm thinking about the sixth,' Jimson said. 'Pharaoh depends on that Turk of his, and Aziz the Turk won't be there just when he needs him. That's the craziest part.'

Brandsteller twiddled the dial of the radio in search of an oasis of recognizable music in the desert of Arab caterwaulings. In the meanwhile Jimson admired the scenery: the peasants at work with their buffaloes under the hazy evening light; canals everywhere breeding little local mists; naked boys stalking birds with their nets or delving for catfish in the mud. 'Beautiful, isn't it? Miraculous. Way I used to think heaven looked when I was a kid.'

'How did you find Kemp?' Brandsteller asked.

'As before. Naïve. That was a great idea of Vickers to bring his wife into this. She certainly has an armlock on him when it comes to extracting the cash. I told him I'd be back for a swim again today, or maybe tomorrow. Thought it might look better that way than if I appeared out of the blue then took off right away. I worked out the way to handle Kemp. He's the kind of guy who likes to believe what he's told.'

It was within an hour of nightfall on a softly foggy evening when they drove into Bahra. Business over for the day, the main street was full of prosperous vegetable merchants who had seated themselves on golden throne-like chairs to have their shoes polished while they dictated a letter to a scribe, or had their blood pressure taken by an itinerant doctor. The dhows were instantly visible, nobly profiled above the mean alleyways crammed into the waterfront. El Rashid was a place where time had stood still, and Jimson much admired such places.

They parked the car among a scrum of street urchins and traipsed down through the mud, hens, and flocks of goats, to the yard. It was a repository, a museum, and a cemetery of old ocean-going ships, abandoned here by men who had not been able to bring themselves to accept the truth that they would go to sea no more, but who had thereafter slowly forgotten their existence. A yellow tide licked at their rotting, barnacle-warted timbers, and they smelled of the ancient pollution of the sea. Shipbuilders were at work with saws and planes to shape planks to be hammered into position in the framework of sambuks built to satisfy the nostalgia of the rich, or for real use by the poorest class of seafaring trader on short voyages along the Red Sea coasts. One of the sambuks, just finished, was already floodlit, and a notice tacked to its honey-coloured flank, prefixed with an affirmation of the vendor's belief in the generosity of God, suggested an approximate price.

They strolled round the newly built ship. 'Eddie,' Jimson said, 'we can relax, we're on business. This is what I was hoping for.'

'Like the boats you saw back in Tripoli, huh?'

'The resemblance is extraordinary,' Jimson said. 'My God, this is a fine-looking boat.'

'Dhows aren't what they were,' Brandsteller said. 'The wood used in the construction for instance. Teak's a thing of the past.'

'It doesn't bother me, so long as it floats. You know there wouldn't be much to alter here apart from fitting a more powerful engine. Any idea what speed you could coax out of it?'

'I happen to have read something about dhow conversions the other day,' Brandsteller said. 'Fitted with the standard 100 h.p. diesel they practically stand still in the water. With a 500 h.p. Cummings, or one of the new Caterpillars this might do fourteen knots. I say *might*.'

'That all?'

'The speed factor is determined by the waterline length and the displacement of the hull,' Brandsteller said. 'As a rough guide you take the square root of the waterline length and multiply it by 1.5—say 1.8 if you're *very* lucky. What we're looking for is a long, narrow boat. Which is what this is.'

'We can check by the pictures tomorrow,' Jimson said, 'but this is so close to a Tripoli tunny-fishing boat that all you'd have to do is hack off a bit here and stick on a bit there to make it identical so far as the radar contour goes. Anything else would be cosmetic. This sambuk could pass itself off as a fishing boat at night. It could come in with the other boats when they're on their way back from their fishing. Fix up the acetylene lights on it they use, and not even the fishermen would know they've got a wolf in their fold. They go out at night to put down their nets and they come in just before dawn. It's a routine they always follow.'

'What you tell me makes me feel somewhat more optimistic than I did,' Brandsteller said. 'We still have to work very fast.'

'A big engine has to be fitted and a bit of carpentry done. Any idea at all how long that might take?'

'It all depends on Parsons,' Brandsteller said. 'Anything's possible in this country if the money's there. If Parsons shows any enthusiasm everything in this shipyard would come to a standstill while they got the boat ready for us. How long would it take? A couple of days? Three at most. It all depends on Parsons.'

The meeting next day with Parsons was a success, although under a show of breezy euphoria Jimson was distracted by a new possibility. He gave Parsons his photographs of the beach and the tunny boats. Parsons showed himself completely satisfied with the way it had all turned out, then handed over a briefcase containing a hundred and twenty new thousand dollar notes, payable to Jimson in advance as agreed, and constituting three quarters of the amount he was to receive, the final payment to be made after the successful conclusion of the operation. Jimson then went off to the quiet hotel he stayed at in Heliopolis, where he took a scalding shower, drank three cups of black coffee in quick succession and settled to think.

Jimson was of the opinion that he would receive no more money from the Agency than the sum he had already been paid, basing this pessimistic view on the Agency's outstandingly poor record in operations of this kind. It was while considering this conclusion that he hit on an idea that might provide financial security and the capital necessary to permit him to exchange his present trade for a calmer way of existence.

His life-style presented a striking anomaly. He did little with the money he made, which had for him hardly more than symbolical value, and he continued at heart to be a man of simple tastes. A rare form of neurotic compulsion, a persistent love affair with danger, had driven Jimson to become what he was, but the excitements that had bound him to his profession were slackening, while the perils remained.

Jimson proposed for himself one last fling, a final spectacular coup. It was calculated to sate whatever remained of a taste for foolhardy adventures, because it would involve a double-cross of the Agency, known to employ dedicated professionals to revenge themselves on double-dealers.

He lay awake most of the night busy with plans for

reshaping his existence. In the morning he visited the seedy offices of the Bolivian Consulate in the maze of streets behind Tahrir Square. The walls were covered with enlarged photographs of the ice-peaks of the Andes, and of Indians in marvellously embroidered costumes engaged in a fiesta, many of them appearing to be drunk.

Jimson wandered from photograph to photograph, smiling happily behind his beard. He had never heard of a criminal extradited from this country, or a fugitive hunted down. 'Beautiful-looking place, isn't it?' he said.

The Consul was at his shoulder. 'Bolivia,' he said, 'is the white man's promised land. You as a British subject would be included in the class of specially desirable immigrants to whom we offer, without payment, fifty hectares of first-class agricultural land. We need you to help fill our vast empty spaces.'

The man was small and bird-like, with an eye that twitched as if about to wink, and a good-natured leer bred in an environment where leers were respectable. 'Are you married, Mr Jimson?'

'Unfortunately, no.'

'In our country it is helpful to have a wife. There are agencies in the capital able to provide girls of good family. There are many to select from.'

'Isn't Bolivia the land of the llama?' Jimson asked.

'Also of the alpaca and many other beautiful animals. Jaguars and deer we have in our forests, many of them. As a sportsman you would obtain many fine trophies.'

'I don't want to kill animals, only watch them,' Jimson said.

All in all, Bolivia seemed as good a place as any in which to pass his declining years. Jimson was weary of the cat-and-mouse game of his life, of unremitting watchfulness, of the night-comers and the men of silence, of seedy, scaled-down versions of violent television adventure, of coups and triumphs booby-trapped with disaster. Age, in a word, had laid its hand on his shoulder.

Sensing his small interest in the prospect of marriage to a

155

young Bolivian lady of good family the Consul returned to the pleasures and rewards of country life in the tropics.

It was a good thing to own a farm, he said, and you could even make some sort of a living growing sugar cane in the lowlands on the government's gift of fifty hectares. To be a rancher, he thought, if one could find a bit of capital, was better. 'Could you put your hand on ten thousand pounds?' he asked.

'I hope so,' Jimson said.

'Twenty maybe?'

'Maybe twenty.'

'With twenty you can buy so much jungle it's going to take you a week to ride around it. You burn the trees down, you plant grass and put 500 head of cattle on it for a start. The government will help you with a credit. In three years you will increase your capital tenfold.'

'It's not the money,' Jimson said. 'It's the way of life.'

'The way of life? Let me explain. After three years you will smell of money. In the morning a servant comes to wake you up with a harp. You will be carried in a chair into church. When you take a stroll in the plaza smoking that big cigar the kids are going to fight to guard your car, and every man you stop to say *buenos días* to, will take off his hat and call you *Patrón*.'

'You make it all sound very attractive,' Jimson said.

He had planned to stay another day in Cairo, then decided there was not enough time, so he took a midday flight back to Malta and caught a Libyan-Arab plane to Tripoli the same afternoon.

Inevitably he was held at the airport because his visa was no longer valid, and led away to the interview room for questioning. Jimson managed to convince the interviewing officer that, visa or no visa, there were most urgent and secret reasons for his return, and the man agreed to his request to be taken to the Ministry of Defence.

The major who saw him listened with no evidence of emotion or even interest to selected facts from a lurid story Jimson was prepared to market, not even raising an eyebrow

156

at a suggested figure of a quarter of a million dollars, put forward in a modest tone that seemed to indicate that scope for negotiation existed.

When Jimson had finished he spoke briefly in Arabic into the house phone and a moment later the brigadier who was Chief Security Defence Officer entered the room.

The brigadier, who had passed through Sandhurst, and was clipped of moustache and manner, asked Jimson to go over his story once again. Jimson scattered his enticing crumbs of information, and the brigadier smiled. As if permission had been requested and granted, the major smiled, too, then the brigadier broke into a hearty laugh, and the major added his brief, subordinate chuckle.

'Tell me, once again,' the brigadier said. 'What was the date on which all this was to take place?'

'The sixth,' Jimson said, puzzled and a little alarmed at the way the thing was going.

'The sixth, I see,' the brigadier said. He got up. 'Well, I don't think there's anything more we need say.'

He spoke in Arabic to the major. 'This man is mad.'

'Yes,' the major said. 'He is mad.'

'An obsessive, but quite harmless. Do we have a signed photograph of the Brother Leader to spare?'

'I can find one.'

'Give it to him. Give him also one hundred dollars. Hold him until the seventh, then send him on his way.'

The major led Jimson away to one of the secure but well-appointed flatlets in the airport in which suspect persons were held pending a decision as to their fate. A half hour later a key turned in the lock and the brigadier let himself in.

'I have been thinking,' he said. 'You spoke of a boat. Can you describe it to me?'

The confident smile moved behind Jimson's beard. 'I can do better than that. I can make an accurate drawing for you.'

'Good. I will give you pencil and paper, and you will draw the boat. Perhaps we can come to an arrangement, after all.'

Chapter Eighteen

There were four more days of waiting to be used up with the threat of the model cell in the model prison never out of the back of Kemp's mind. He would take incoming telephone calls, but outgoing calls could not be made.

Mike phoned. 'It seems you made it?'

'Well, yes. It isn't exactly what I'd call bail. I'm far from a free man, but it isn't too bad.'

'I'd like to come round.'

'Sorry, visitors are banned.'

'The Embassy is doing all it can. I wouldn't expect too much, though.'

'I don't.'

'Craddock's gone,' Mike said. 'He took off without a word to anyone. I went round to see him at the Compound yesterday, and found the house empty.'

'Any theories?' Kemp asked.

'He probably saw trouble ahead. They always catch up with you sooner or later when you're in booze,' Mike said. 'Wonder they never pounced on him before.'

'May have had their reasons,' Kemp said. He and Sayed hung up together. 'I am sorry, Mr Kemp,' Sayed said. 'Be sure I am not a police informer. These matters are regarded by me as confidential.'

'Thank you.'

'Shall we play chess now?'

'If you feel like it.' They played a game in which Kemp was demolished in a few moves. They were no good as car drivers, he thought; not much better at growing their own food; but they could certainly play chess.

'Excuse me, Mr Kemp. I was obliged to hear of your feeling

that your freedom has been taken from you. We can go anywhere you like together.'

'Let's go to Leptis,' Kemp said.

'*Marhaba*. Okay by me.'

They drove hair-raisingly in Sayed's Datsun to Leptis Magna, but collided with a camel resting in the road on their way back, and the owner and his friends showered the car with stones. The incident brought them closer together.

'These are very ignorant countrymen,' Sayed said. 'We shall rescue them from their ignorance. Soon not a camel will remain in our country.'

'All the same, we had a great day,' Kemp assured him.

'If I am to tell you the truth, I do not care much for things of the past. I do not care for ruins.'

'The marshalling yards round York Way are more your scene.'

'It was pleasant to walk in the evening. I lived with my friends under the railway arches in Hearn Street. You will know this place. There was always movement, always noise. It was a place of the future. My great hope is to go back to London.'

Mike phoned again next day. 'Just to tell you Claire tracked me down for news of you. I told her as much as I thought she ought to know about what's happened. She took it quite well and sends her love and good wishes, as do all your friends. Oh yes, she told me not to worry about the house. Everything's been settled. Be nice if you could talk to her.'

'I wish I could. I've disappointed her so often about coming home. This could mean another delay, and there have been so many.'

Shackled by passive routines, the days wound down slowly. They read, swam, listened to Sayed's collection of pop music, played chess with Kemp always the loser. The view seawards was always dreamily pacific. Country women from the Arabian nights kept indolent watch on goats chewing away the last of the marram grass. The sea lay benumbed under its autumn calm. Early in the evening the fishermen chanted their prayers before dragging their boats down to the water and lighting their acetylene lamps. Kemp went to bed early, and by the time he did so their lights were twinkling across a third of the horizon.

On the night of the fifth, shortly after midnight, Kemp was awakened by the sound of tramping feet in the street below. This was followed by a familiar rumble and clank of armoured vehicles, interrupted suddenly by a heavy crash followed by frantic cries. He rolled out of bed to reach the window. A few torches were bobbing and flashing in the street, and by their light he saw soldiers clustered round the hole in the road by his door from which the rear end of a tank protruded. It was a scene of confusion, of shouted orders and counter-orders, of fury and despair. An MP with a white bucket helmet was trying to clear the traffic jam and release a snarl-up of tanks and half-tracks which had formed.

He crossed the room to the window looking out over the beach, where he saw a few lights dodging will-o-the-wisp style among the scrub. Then for a split second a searchlight of tremendous power fanned its beam across the shore, revealing among the frosted whiteness of sand and the shadows peaked from the bushes a trail of soldiers burdened like leaf-cutter ants, with gear unloaded from supply lorries which they were carrying towards the sea.

Sayed knocked at the door, fully dressed, and wincing with agitation. 'Mr Kemp, we must go now. We must go to a house in another place. A car is waiting to take us. I'll be with you in a moment.'

Kemp dressed while Sayed stood watchfully at the door, then they went down to a patrol car with a revolving light and an excited policeman at the wheel. A recovery vehicle came blustering through to deal with the tank. The police car's headlight came on as they moved off, and Kemp noted the presence of special assault troops among the soldiers, sprouting a camouflage of tamarisk branches which seemed to him to have rendered them more conspicuous than they would otherwise have been.

'Tell me, Sayed, do you have any idea what this is all about?'

'Mr Kemp, I am as you say, a cog in the machine. They tell me nothing.'

160

Chapter Nineteen

At Bahra the problem had remained that of time. Three days were required to obtain and fit the more powerful engine. In the meanwhile much of the sambuk's superstructure was removed and fishing lamps installed on its bows. Parsons and Brandsteller decided that no visible armament could be added to the boat in the way of cannon or rocket-launchers. Even if camouflaged they might attract the suspicions of reconnaissance aircraft in Libyan waters. Moreover all that really mattered was for the vessel to be able to mingle with and pass unnoticed among others of its kind.

The Turk Aziz arrived with his hookah, his prayer-beads, the personal standard brought from Mecca on which the name of Allah had been embroidered in gold thread a thousand times and—since he was a hypochondriac—a medicine chest containing a hundred or so remedies for the more common ailments. Aziz's reputation for dealing with the slightest act of insubordination by personally blowing the offender's brains out was enough to keep the thirty-two ferocious militiamen enlisted in Lebanon in a state of dumb acquiescence.

Hawi, in Tripoli, remained silent after his one radio signal. For reasons of security there would be no attempt to make radio contact with him until the early hours of the sixth, and he would be given no knowledge of the place chosen for the landing until the assault force was actually ashore. The plan agreed upon by the two American agents, Aziz, and his second in command, was that the sambuk should sail from Bahra at dawn on the fourth of October, entering Libyan waters at nightfall on the same day. Aziz's lieutenant, Golu, also a Turk, had attended a security course at a US base in Western Germany and, influenced by this, had two fair-skinned members of the company disguise themselves as yachtsmen with peaked caps and binoculars as they left port shortly before 5 a.m. There was nobody up at that time to see them go.

The weather, after the passage of the first of the autumn storms, was exceptionally fine and clear. Just before sundown a stop was made at Bardia to fill up the fuel tanks. Defying Aziz's prohibition, one of the mercenaries took this opportunity to slip ashore in search of liquor. He was caught and dragged back, and Aziz broke his jaw with a blow of his fist on which he wore a knuckle-duster made with dental gold from the mouths of the dead recovered after the Sinai battle.

That night they kept close to the curving upsweep of the coast of Cyrenaica and by morning they were in the opening of the great sack of the Gulf of Sirte, heading for Taworga. There were Italian boats from Palermo fishing illegally in the Gulf. They passed a patched-up floating coffin from Tunis over-laden with cement and iron bars, and while still out of sight of Misurata a Libyan fighter came up out of the horizon, its underside aglitter with evening reflections, for a quick look at them before turning off, convinced by their lateen sail, and heading back to its base.

Night overtook them as they passed Misurata, and at two in the morning Tripoli showed in a sallow glow along the southern horizon. The navigator pinpointed for Aziz their position on his chart. They had arrived. But where there should have been a mile-wide crescent of boats anchored over the fishing bank, drawing the fish into the nets with their lights, there was nothing to be seen but an empty sea under a wasted moon.

Primitive fishermen the world over—none more so than the tunny-fishers of North Africa—are the victims of a harsh regime of superstition; wary observers of signs and omens to be studied and dreams to be interpreted, if damage to the fishing prospects is to be avoided. On the previous day, after an afternoon nap taken just before the boats put to sea for the night's work, the *Raïs*, captain of the fleet, reported a dream that they had taken a man-faced sea monster in their nets. The decision to call off that night's fishing was unanimous. No one had noticed the *Raïs*'s brief meeting before this announcement with a stranger in city clothes, who had called him aside for a low-voiced conference. The boats, drawn up on the beach, were ritually purified by the perfumed smoke of acacia wood, after which the fishermen drank tea, told stories, then covered their faces against injury by lunar light before going to sleep.

For the expedition there was nothing to be done but to anchor and wait tediously, with the slow bleeding away of optimism and confidence, for the dawn. Aziz's instincts had warned him against this adventure from the moment of its conception in the President's brain. He had gone along with it reluctantly, persuaded only to do so because it would have been impossible for him to say no to a man who was not only his master, in the old-fashioned feudal sense of the word, but his only friend. The Koran, in one of its suras, expressly forbade subterfuge, even in warfare, and there was too much subterfuge, too much trickery in this affair for a man of Aziz's training and temperament, predisposed at all times in favour of a frontal assault upon a visible enemy.

Shortly before dawn he gave the order to make for the coast, in the hope, at first light, of identifying the beach from enlargements of Jimson's photographs. In this, to Aziz's relief, they were successful, and they anchored again a quarter of a mile offshore in sight of what were unmistakably the tower, Kemp's villa, and even the tunny boats, drawn up in a neat line on the beach, clear of the water.

The radio operator, ordered at this point to make the attempt to contact Hawi, was instantly successful, and the pre-arranged code phrases were exchanged signifying that all was in order. It was a circumstance that did little to alleviate Aziz's increasing doubts, but they were too far committed now to withdraw. Aziz gulped down four aspirins, and ordered the mercenaries into the rubber dinghies in the hope that by the time they had paddled ashore the convoy of cars, to be provided by Hawi to carry them to their target in the heart of the City, would come into sight.

The dinghies were beached just as the dawn striped the sky through the skeleton of an unfinished building across the coast road. The dogs who had picked up an alien human odour began to bark, and the sound jostled the mercenaries into a tighter group full of nervous undecided movements, like sheep herded to the entrance of a pen.

Golu stood at Aziz's side, a small man overbalanced by the weight of his machine gun. '*Ma yeta'al*', he said. In a language which had developed no future tense it could have meant either 'he isn't coming', or 'he won't come'.

'*La, ma yeta'al.*' Shamir's agreement contained a verdict.

Golu had smuggled a young lover aboard who refused to be separated from him, and this boy, Emirdag, now made the first doubtful appearance. Trailing at his heels came a self-appointed spokesman of the mercenaries, exhaling defeatism like a foul breath. 'The Phalangists want to go back, Captain.'

'Too late, too late,' Aziz said, and for once his tone was not overbearing. In that very moment he had detected a sly movement in the middle of broken ground ahead, just beyond the crisp frontier of sand—the beginnings of the deadly, phallic emergence of a missile launcher from its silo.

'You have time for a cigarette, no more,' Aziz said, his voice reduced almost to a whisper. The threat they lay under imposed its own brand of democracy, for there were no more orders to be given or obeyed.

The upthrust of the missile launcher was halted, Aziz heard a thin, hooting cry he took to be the word of command, a feathered meteorite whooshed overhead, then the blast of a great explosion at their backs ruffled the hair in the nape of his neck and tugged at the sleeves of his uniform. Turning quickly he caught a glimpse of the last of the sambuk's destruction, its parts displayed for an instant in suspension, like those of a constructional toy, before splashing into the sea.

The firing began, but there could be no retaliation or defence against the well-prepared and perfectly concealed enemy that awaited the landing party. Those of the mercenaries who survived the first volleys threw away their arms and ran for the dinghies only to see them deflated by invisible sharp-shooters before they could be reached. What followed was a leisurely cat-and-mouse hunting down and extermination of screaming, blubbering fugitives, whose ludicrous antics as they ran, limped, crawled or dragged themselves from place to place in a hopeless attempt to escape the bullets, evoked no more than laughter from their executioners.

Aziz, Golu and Emirdag, at first overlooked in the manhunt, crouched together behind an upturned boat. Golu had taken Emirdag's hand. 'What now?' Emirdag asked.

'You have no sons to bless, but remember your father and mother, and think of God,' Aziz said. No close member of his own family remained alive. He called upon God, and then his friend the President. 'Oh Anwar, what will become of you now?'

The setting was one for a last stand, a national tradition dear to Turkish hearts. As fighters the Turks were uninspired but stubborn, and there were few peasant shacks in the hard Anatolian land without a coloured print on the wall showing some Turkish army lad, mortally wounded, his soul in the form of a small bird taking flight from his mouth, surrounded by the numerous corpses, Russian, British or Greek, he had personally accounted for. In the absence of any hope of victory, it was seen as a model outcome of an encounter. The mercenaries ran and died, but the Turks would stand and die, because this was their custom.

Every kind of weapon was trained on the boat but the attackers were in no hurry. A single machine-gun burst drilled a line of holes high up through the boat's timbers. There was a pause, and then a three-inch shell fired from a roof-top carried half the bows away. Emirdag was struck in the stomach by a small piece of shrapnel and Golu's right eye was damaged by a flying splinter of wood, but all three men were on their feet.

'Let us sing,' Aziz said. Traditionally this was the moment to break into a death chant, but times had changed, customs were dying fast, and none of them could remember any of the old tunes or the words.

165

That year a Lebanese pop song was all the rage in the Middle East. 'If you can't think of anything better, what's wrong with *Lama El Walad Yenam*?' Aziz asked. It was about a lover who waits for his girl's baby to go to sleep before he sneaks into her room, and it could not have been less appropriate for the occasion, but they all knew it well, so they made a start.

Chapter Twenty

All the assemblage, the ambassadors, the foreign notabilities, the diplomats and the journalists, bowed as the President, with his entourage, entered and took his seat. They stood again for the reading from the Koran, then clapped their hands over their ears, as the mortars exploded overhead to release a blizzard of miniature parachutes carrying tiny pictures of the President, and the national flag.

The President settled himself, took out his pipe and began to puff on his scented tobacco. He was as trim as ever in his splendid uniform, whereas the ministers flanking him wore bulletproof vests, adding an unnatural bulk under their braided and bemedalled tunics. It was a great public occasion, the anniversary of victory, and the President, sweating profusely, showed his pleasure and excitement as he always did. He craved adulation, an excuse to show himself in public. He loved to make a show of throwing caution to the winds, as he had done today by ordering his eight security guards, clinging to the sides and back of his limousine, to dismount before they were in view of the reviewing stand. It was his wish to appear to his people, his children, protected only by God.

On the previous day the museum had been suddenly cleared for a surprise presidential visit, and the President had detached himself from his friends—some of them bewildered and a little uneasy—to stand in contemplation before the famous statuette of Tut-ankh-amun, shown as Horus, the falcon-god, carrying the lance and chain to subdue Evil in the form of a hippopotamus lurking in a marsh. The President was celebrated for his trance-like silences that had been known sometimes to come upon him even in conversation with foreign dignitaries.

Shortly after the episode at the museum, while discussing the arrangements for next day's parade with a party of senior officers, he was seized with such a silence. Half an hour passed before the discussion was resumed, and for a moment the President appeared to have forgotten why the meeting had been called. 'Are you familiar with the legend of Osiris?' he asked them. 'Horus, the Pharaoh, is his son. He reigns in the world of the living while the murdered Osiris is resurrected to rule in the kingdom of the dead.' The President stared into the ring of perplexed faces with absolute seriousness. 'When his time comes, Horus, too, is murdered to become one with Osiris in the underworld. Such is a pharaoh's fate if he is to become a god.'

Brandsteller found Parsons perched in isolation at the back of the stand, which was less than half full.

'Still no news?' Parsons asked.

'None.'

'We should have heard something hours ago. It actually hurts me to have to wait like this.'

'The radio blackout's still in operation,' Brandsteller said. 'It's a sure sign of a major shake-up or a political crisis. They're broadcasting martial music, that's all. The longer it lasts the better, from our point of view. It could be they're deciding the best way to break the bad news to the country. I don't feel unhopeful.'

'I wish I could share your optimism,' Parsons said.

'We have to know soon.'

'Maybe I'm abnormally sensitive to atmospheres,' Parsons said. 'There's a feeling in the air here I don't like, plus an absolute lack of security. Were you checked for a pass when you came in just now?'

'The guard was talking to a couple of his friends. I walked straight in and nobody stopped me.'

'When I came in there was a guy taking up the slack in his

belt at the gate. I'd deliberately left off my badge. I asked him if he wanted to see my pass and he waved me straight through. Where are Aziz's famous Special Staff? Did you see any sign of them?'

'None. Aziz isn't around so they haven't bothered to show up.'

'We paid two million dollars for a Sikorsky CH—53 armoured helicopter to handle this kind of scene. Where is it? Where are the sharpshooters they should have put up there on all those roofs?'

'There's supposed to be a police cordon thrown right round this area,' Brandsteller said. 'You won't believe this, but literally—I mean *literally*—I just saw a horse and cart being driven through it. You can walk out of this stand and buy a coke and come back any time you want. I can see a woman sitting within twenty feet of the President who's a well known hooker. Who's to know she hasn't got a gun in that handbag?'

'If Aziz isn't here, why should these guys bother? Can you explain to me why the President let him go?'

'That's something you and I will never understand.'

The first of the planes, Mirage 5-E fighters, came over in formation, too low for safety, trailing smoke fired in colours, and blasting away their words. The President twisted in his seat, smiling and with sweat beading from every pore, to follow them through his binoculars. 'Mach 1.7 ... better manoeuvrability ... tighter on the turn,' Brandsteller muttered to himself, unheard before a moment of peace descended.

Brandsteller raced to use up the silence threatened by the next wave of jets. His eye had settled on the ugly modernistic Tomb of the Unknown Soldier facing them across the parade route. 'What was the idea of building that goddam pyramid?'

'How should I know? I suppose it's a kind of national symbol.'

'They all say he's figuring on being buried there himself. It's part of his way of thinking.'

'He's concerned with the hereafter,' Parsons said. 'I can see no objection to that.'

'The nation laid out a total of 10.75 millions for that heap of building material,' Brandsteller said. 'They used the lowest grade concrete under the stone facing. Scooped the sand for it out of some goddam river-bed.'

'There's only the Nile,' Parsons said.

'I'm referring to dried up wadis, which are plentiful.'

'What does it matter, Eddie? You expect too much. Everything's a racket.'

'His own brother was supposed to be involved.'

'That, too, wouldn't surprise me.'

More jets screamed overhead and Parsons winced and shook off the sound like a dog ridding itself of water. 'You did tell them to get a message up to us if any news came through?' he asked Brandsteller.

'I did. Want me to go and check again?'

'Might as well. I can't stand this suspense.'

Brandsteller went off and Parsons watched the scene moodily. Despite all the din it was a dispirited affair. A fat cat from Kuwait seated two rows behind the President had actually fallen asleep and an official from the Italian Embassy was licking at an ice-cream surreptitiously behind a cupped hand. How did he manage to come by the ice-cream when he had not left his seat? It must have been handed down from a vendor who had managed to slip in and conceal himself among the unimportant visitors standing at the back. The only security guard in sight anywhere was standing in the tail of a queue waiting to use a latrine under the stand. Parsons noted that a party of schoolgirls who had been lined up behind a fence to wave flags, then left unattended, were wandering off. The crowds had kept away, and perhaps it was a good thing they had.

A scuffle of footsteps behind him made him turn, and Brandsteller was back, baring his teeth at the corners of his mouth in a way that Parsons knew could equally signal elation or despair. He fell into his seat while Parsons drew his right hand down his cheeks in an habitual gesture originally intended to smooth out the lines of intense anxiety produced by such occasions.

'What happened?' Parsons asked.

'The news just came through,' Brandsteller said.

'Hold it before you tell me any more. I want it in one word. Yes, or no?'

'No,' Brandsteller said.

'We blew it again?'

'Pharaoh blew it. He didn't give us time.'

'*We* blew it. How about the assault party? Wiped out, were they?'

'We don't have any more details. The Gadfly spoke to the nation a few minutes ago, and it was the usual thing. The routine denial they always put out. Nothing has happened or will happen, because the people will always prevail. That's all the official news we'll ever hear.'

'It was a massacre, make no mistake about that,' Parsons said. He massaged his sagging cheeks. 'I had this premonition,' he said. 'I knew it was bound to happen. Of course there wasn't enough time. As soon as I heard one of his religious fanatics was mixed up in it, this feeling came over me. This is the Middle East. We're trained to deal with devious situations, but there's nothing in our training helps much with Egypt.'

'Things are going to be a lot worse without Aziz to lean on,' Brandsteller said.

'I've just had a terrible thought,' Parsons said. 'Perhaps Pharaoh would have been happy for it to happen this way. Maybe he'll even be happy to get the man off his back. He's like a kid who wants to put on a uniform with a row of medals and ribbons, and go around with a toy gun to show himself off, and Aziz used to hold him back. Now he's going to be able to do what he goddam pleases. . . . Listen, how much longer is this going on? I want to get away from here and go somewhere I can think.'

'We could go now. What's to stop us?'

'You'd better stay. Might look bad if we both pull out. Come round to the hotel as soon as you get away. We have to decide where we go from here.'

'Be round right away,' Brandsteller said. His intention was

to make his escape as soon as Parsons was out of sight. He could feel the throb of his nerves through the terrific uproar of the Czech MIGs overhead.

The details of the scene below, the marching, cheering, saluting, flag-waving, hardly registered in his preoccupied brain, but he thanked God it was all slackening, falling away, grinding to an end. All the impressive exhibits had been used up. Now it was the scrapings of the barrel, soldiers in plain ill-fitting uniforms, veteran trucks towing obsolete guns. He came out of his trance, got up to go, intercepted the shocked side-glance of an Egyptian neighbour, forced himself to sit down again.

It had turned into a really ragged performance, he noted dully. One truck towing a gun had actually pulled out of line and stalled. A soldier jumped down and began to march towards the reviewing stand, at which the President and the two mnisters flanking him rose to their feet, ready apparently to take a salute. Would this business never come to an end?

Three more soldiers dropped from the truck and came running, and Brandsteller, alerted now to an instinctive preview of what was about to happen, watched with a curious detachment while the first soldier lobbed a hand-grenade over the barrier, and the others levelled their guns and opened fire.

The stampede to escape the bullets cleared the seats all round, leaving Brandsteller to sit alone, his body rigid, anchored by the grip of his fingers on the sides of his chair. Where seconds ago the President and his aides had stood, bodies were now heaped in grotesque positions. Shoes, hats and handbags were strewn among the upturned chairs. Men were dragging themselves painfully up the stairs, others lay in comfortable attitudes of deep sleep. The shooting died away. The last grenade burst in a small red flash from which a mourning wraith spread, then vanished. Now the guards were back, shouting and waving their pistols, and for the first time that day Brandsteller saw Aziz's men in their purple berets.

He sat there, saw the assassins or presumed assassins captured, led away or dragged senseless to waiting police cars. Medical teams arrived to swab and bandage the wounds of groaning victims. Blood was mopped up from chair seats and the rich carpet that so nearly matched its colour. Without turning his head, Brandsteller saw the President released from the bodies that held him down, lifted to a stretcher, then the stretcher rushed to a helicopter that had just landed. A great tragedy had been staged as if for his private view, but the viewing of it had left him drained. A man in uniform came up, patted him on the shoulder and gestured to him to go. Brandsteller got up and stumbled after the man to the stairs. Until this moment exhaustion had bereft him almost of the power to think, but now the full realization of what had happened struck him like a tidal wave. I'm washed up. Finished, he told himself. Now Pharaoh's gone, what use am I to anyone?

They flew the President to the military hospital where eleven doctors and surgeons waited in line—some of them trembling—as if to be received in audience by the great man now recumbent on the table. A prayer was said before they cut away the ribs to lay bare the anarchy, the confusion, the riddle of ruined organs drowning in a morass of blood that had ceased to flow. There were puzzles here without solution for those who fell to work to inject stimulants, give transfusions, carry out electric shock treatment, massage the heart, manipulate the suction tubes that drew clotted blood and air from the larynx, the trachea and the cavities of the chest.

Not a single man, among the eleven extending his professional talents to the utmost in this operation, deceived himself that what he was doing had more than a ceremonial purpose, a sterile magical rite from which his intelligence compelled him to withhold belief.

After a half hour, as if by common consent, there was a pause for the exchange of glances full of meaning. Artificial respiration kept the air wheezing and bubbling through the lungs that had been pierced by so many bullets and splinters of bone, but the heart had not restarted, there was no trace—nor had ever been—of reflexes, or response to light in the wide open eyes.

The senior surgeon, who had recorded a drop in bodily temperature, stepped back from the table and raised his hand, and his subordinates straightened themselves to leave whatever was occupying them. 'Only God can live for ever,' the senior surgeon said, and there was a murmur from some of the others of '*Allah akbar*'.

Pharaoh had become Osiris.

Chapter Twenty-one

Kemp's sleep in the house they had moved to on the far side of the town was disturbed by a heavy explosion followed by distant gunfire. This he reported in the morning to Sayed, who appeared surprised and claimed to have heard nothing. Shortly after, two serious-faced Arabs called on Sayed. Their over-politeness, even the carefully knotted ties and abnormally high polish on their shoes, suggested to Kemp that there was something in the air. They bowed their way into the room, and gave him the tips of their fingers. A formal conversation about the unseasonal rains threatened to develop but Kemp could see that they were anxious to get him out of the way, so he excused himself and left them to their low-voiced confabulation with Sayed while he occupied himself in the adjoining room.

After a short time he heard them leave. A moment later Sayed came into the room, exuding a carefully prepared nonchalance.

'I spoke to my friends about the disturbance we suffered last night. This was a routine army exercise. That is all.' He laughed like a trader hoping to distract attention from an article's inferior quality. 'You were so sure that there was an attempt at a coup, but you were wrong. Everything is quite normal and very calm.'

'Of course it is,' Kemp said. 'I ought to be used to routine exercises by this time. The gunfire I heard must have been all part of it. Will we be going back to my old villa when the exercises are over?'

'To be frank, Mr Kemp, I am not considered important enough to be told anything until the last minute.'

In the early afternoon the dancing started. It was a spectacle of a kind Kemp had never before experienced in all the years among the Arabs. First the men came out into the street, and then a few women began to make a cautious appearance, although keeping, as ever, to themselves. The men linked arms to form lines and began a simple, almost sedate dance, of the kind tourists are sometimes invited to take part in in Greek tavernas. One, two, three, kick. One, two, three, kick. The thudding of drums had drawn them out of the half-finished, high-rise buildings, and the packing-case shacks in which they lived, and they were joined by car-drivers and their passengers who could push no further ahead with their cars, and had abandoned them to mingle with the crowds. One, two, three, kick. One, two, three, kick. Some of the young men had broken loose and begun to gyrate and leap. Women in garish, shapeless dresses ululated, beating their lips with the palms of their hands in the way they expressed either extremes of joy or of grief.

'Sayed, what on earth's going on?'

'They are celebrating the victory of the Arab people, Mr Kemp. In this way they show their feelings. The news has just reached us. Our great Egyptian enemy has been removed by the people's justice.'

'Assassinated, you mean? The President?'

'Yes, he is truly dead. He is gone from this world.'

'And is this something to be so wildly excited about? Will it really make any difference to any of you in the long run?'

'In life this man divided our people. Now they are gathered together again. This false shepherd has been taken from the flock.' Sayed's command of colloquial English had succumbed to his excitement. Now he fumbled to translate his thoughts from the Arabic.

'So things are looking up for you?'

'Mr Kemp, the future is bright as we have never seen it before.'

Kemp laughed. They were standing just inside the doorway of the villa watching the goings-on in the street. Kemp glanced up for a moment, and Sayed followed his eye. The space between the door-top and ceiling bore the remnant of an inscription put there by the Fascist hierarch who had once owned the house. *Bisogna credere, obbedire, combattere,* the full inscription had once exhorted the family and its guests, and the Arab who had taken over had seen no reason to expunge more than the last two words, leaving what was in accordance with his own viewpoint: *Bisogna credere*—we must believe.

'There is something,' Kemp said, 'to be said for opium.'

The drums were tugging at Sayed's nerve-strings, and his eyes had lost their focus. 'Let us join the people in their celebration,' he said.

They went out into the wide, crack-surfaced street, now scuffled by so many dancing feet. Hundreds of Arabs were dancing. Whatever their elation, they wore serious faces. Men with sticks ran among the dancers slashing out at evil spirits. There was a mood of growing intoxication, a solemn frenzy, of mass entrancement, and Kemp found himself infected by the excitement.

He followed Sayed and found himself drawn, hardly knowing how it had come about, into a line of dancers. His left arm was entwined through Sayed's and his right through that of a man in a blue boiler suit wearing a dock worker's badge. An old hump-back with rolling eyes and a foam-flecked moustache leaped and capered like a mountain goat in front of them, beating out the time with his stick. One, two, three, kick. One, two, three, kick. Kemp heard himself laugh a little wildly. The drums were thumping in his ears, and through the drum-beats came the piercing joy-sorrow outcry of the women circling with hips bouncing under bunched-up muslin on the periphery of his vision.

Again and again dancers advancing from the other direction broke through their line, and they formed rank again with new partners. Sayed had detached himself, whirling like a dervish till he passed out of sight, and soon the street had changed, and all the faces with it.

In a moment when he, Kemp, had been freed by a collision of dancers, a fat man with tiny eyes and a ragged, knowing smile had come bounding from one of the many stranded cars to grab Kemp's hand. They were dragged forward together for a few yards when the line moved on again, and then he, too, was gone.

Suddenly whatever power it was, whatever upthrust of the instinct, frenzy, exultation, compulsion or hysteria that had seized on the crowd, had burned itself out. The dancers stopped all together, as if some clockwork mechanism operating their limbs had broken down. The drums and the shrill voices of the women were silenced, and the old men threw down their sticks and went off. A mysterious adhesive that had created this crowd had dissolved and it instantly broke up into individuals, each anxious to go about his own business. Car drivers, suddenly impatient, started up their engines and pushed forward, fingers on the buttons of their horns, dispersing the last desultory groups. Kemp found himself alone.

Not quite alone, for one of the cars immobilized until this moment crept down the street towards him and pulled up again. It was a veteran Oldsmobile garishly repainted and down on its springs, a taxi of the pre-Toyota epoch, of the kind now rarely seen. The driver, hauling down the cracked window, called to him, 'Ya musafir, ila ein? Where to, O traveller?' as any taxi-driver might have done.

So this, Kemp understood, was to be his salvation, the way of escape that had been opened to him. He crossed over to the car and the driver held open the nearside door, and Kemp climbed in and lowered himself into the collapsed seat, recognizing as he did so the man who had reached for his hand in the dance. The man thrust a big dimpled paw into the opening of his shirt and brought out a packet which he placed in Kemp's hand. Opening it, Kemp found his passport taken from him at the time of his arrest, and a scrap of paper. 'This man will take you to Bukimash. Inshallah, we shall meet again.'

Bukimash? The name was unfamiliar, outlandish even among Arab place names, yet it seemed to Kemp that he must have heard of it. His experiences in dealing with the Arabs had convinced him that Dr Ahmed could be expected to hold to his side of the bargain, and there had been plenty of time to speculate as to how his escape was most likely to be arranged. In the past many fugitive Libyans who had fallen foul of their radical new government had crossed the land frontiers of the country into Tunisia, Algeria, Niger or Chad. They had simply packed their bags and taken a bus or taxi to Malut, ten miles from the frontier, or Ghaddames which was actually on it, and paid a guide to escort them across and point out their way to the nearest road on the other side.

Later the government had closed these easy bolt holes, built an electrified fence and patrolled the area with frontier guards who had acquired a reputation for meting out rough and instant justice to escapers, under the assumption that they were spies. Further south a trackless desert assumed the function of the electrified fence and it was not until Barka, 400 miles to the south, at the centre of a web of camel routes, that it was possible to cross over into Algeria. Even so this was a hazardous business, with its attendant dangers of being murdered by tribesmen or even overwhelmed by a sandstorm. Kemp had heard of more than one political refugee who had reached Barka, then passed beyond it into oblivion. Better almost, Kemp thought, if offered this grim journey as the only alternative to captivity, to settle for the model prison, and hope for a change of government, or the government's change of heart.

But crashing through the potholes of the city's outskirts Kemp soon realized to his profound relief that he was not to be exposed to any desert adventure, for at the main crossroads the driver took the turning leading to the coast road. It was at that moment that Kemp remembered Bukimash as the last settlement before the Mediterranean end of the frontier with Tunisia, where a miserable sprawl of fishermen's huts attracted expatriate photographers in search of pockets of the steadily vanishing picturesque.

A half-hour after leaving the city they skirted the ruins of Sabratha, and within the hour they were at Bukimash, in the angle of its protective spit of sand. Here fishermen were mending their nets and, watching them, the only other human presence on the beach, a man sat on a camp chair under the shade of an umbrella stuck into the sand. The driver leaned across to release a loop of wire securing the door, and Kemp pushed it open and got out, and the man under the umbrella stood up. He was clad in a Hungarian linen suit of the latest importation, worn with an open-necked *chemise grand sport,* and Italian shoes, and he walked to meet Kemp in the stiff manner of a top official, bowing slightly before holding out his hand. 'Mr Kemp, our mutual friend Dr Ahmed told me you would be coming here. I understand that you will join me for a little fishing trip.' He gestured smilingly towards the men busy with their nets. 'These gentlemen will show us where the fish are to be found. They tell me that the prospects are good.' He paused. 'How are your funds?'

'Ample,' Kemp said.

'Travellers' cheques?'

'Yes. And some dinars.'

'You cannot change the travellers' cheques before Tunis. You had better let me give you dollars for the dinars. You will need cash to buy a bus ticket and food.'

Chapter Twenty-two

Two hours later Kemp waded ashore and into the different world of Tunisia where a kind of enchantment covering unchanged vistas of land and sea assured him that Libya had been left behind. Pulled in by the roadside two hundred yards away from him were a motor-home with an extended awning and satellite tents. Young men and women, their skins the colour of the ochrous earth, sprawled out on sun-loungers, glasses within easy reach.

Soaked with sea water to the tops of his thighs, the sand and water sluicing from his shoes, but almost mad with euphoria, Kemp scrambled over the low rocks towards them. A bronzed young Adonis got up smiling. These people were speaking French but Kemp recognized them as true internationals, citizens of the world-state of pleasure, human beings of a quite different order from expatriates, who had come here in pursuit of vanishing summer at the southern limits of civilization as they knew it.

The Frenchman showed no trace of surprise that Kemp should have appeared so suddenly as he had done, out of the sea.

'*Bonjour,*' Kemp began. '*Savez vous s'il y a un autobus qui passe par ici?*'

'A bus? There is a bus tonight from Ben Gardan.'

A second young man came up, moving gracefully as a panther. '*Vous voulez une bière?*'

'*Merci, vous êtes très gentil.*'

The young women had stopped caressing their shiny skin with creamed fingertips. Two heads were turned towards him with beautiful indifference. 'Where are you going?' the first man said.

'Tunis.'

'Ben Gardan is ten kilometres from here. Let me give you a lift.'

'That would be extremely kind.'

The Frenchman put him down at the bus station at Ben Gardan, where there were flushing toilets and they sold Coca-Cola and cold beer for foreigners. Kemp's nerves were tingling with exultation. He wandered round the souvenir shops admiring the trash they offered for sale, and smiling at people, some of whom smiled back while others looked quickly away. There was a restaurant, too, offering migratory larks grilled on charcoal. He sat down at a table but got up and went out before the waiter came. Excitement had taken away his appetite.

The bus went on time. He fell back into the close, soft embrace of his seat and went to sleep, awakened only briefly by stops at small towns full of fireflies and perfumed by meat cooking on spits.

By six-thirty in the morning they were in Tunis, with a rose-petalled dawn spreading out of the sea. Kemp took a taxi to the Grand Hôtel du Lac, the mausoleum of a splendid past, where all the staff remembered or pretended to remember him. The Tunisians, devoid of ambition or fear, were the most affable of the peoples of North Africa, and everywhere he was received with soft smiles. There were elderly men in the lobby in embroidered waistcoats and the voluminous pleated trousers of the last century, and the head porter was uniformed like a janissary in the army of Abdul the Damned. Kemp knew that as soon as the coast was clear this man would bear down on him with immense dignity with an offer of an amorous encounter. There was a shortage of rooms, said the Assistant Manager, but one would always be found for Kemp. How long would he be staying? Kemp told him possibly not more than one night, and the Assistant Manager asked to be advised as soon as possible if there were any change in his plans. Not an eyebrow had been raised at Kemp's bedraggled appearance, his unshaven cheeks, or the fact that he was without baggage.

Kemp bought shaving gear, a shirt and a newspaper at the shop, and went up to his room. He wanted an excuse to give money away, to be able to include others in his good fortune, and tipped the lift-boy five dollars. He rang for the valet, handed him his suit to be brushed and his shoes to be cleaned, then took a bath, wrapped himself in a towel and glanced at the excited headlines in the English language paper. LAST MOMENTS OF A PRESIDENT. WHO WERE THE TRUE ASSASSINS? There was a small item of Libyan news on an inside page. *It was denied in Tripoli today, for the second time this year, that an attempted coup against the government had been crushed. The situation in the capital was described as normal.*

The valet was back. Kemp gave him ten dollars, dressed, and went down to breakfast. There were no religious prejudices here and a deferential waiter was ready with the bacon and eggs a non-Muslim guest was expected to prefer. Although he did not know the man Kemp could not resist asking him in Arabic after his family and affairs, a civility to which the waiter responded with gratitude.

It was now nine o'clock, local time—one hour in advance of England. Kemp decided to put off ringing home to give Claire time to be up and about. His plan for the day was simple and satisfactory. Having phoned home he intended to rest until midday, when he would take a taxi over to the Medina and lunch at the Daban Abdallah, considered by some the finest restaurant in North Africa. After that he promised himself a quiet nostalgic stroll through the marvellous crooked alleyways around the restaurant where, protected by custom, ignorance and poverty, so many vestiges of things past, so many sights, sounds and odours, so much superstition, piety and resignation contrived to exist.

In the evening, provided his strength held out, he might telephone a Tunisian journalist contact of old, and invite himself to dinner *en famille*. The first day of freedom was to be dedicated to relaxation, the working of the tensions of

Libya out of his system. All things concerning the future were to be resolutely put out of mind. There were many things to be decided, among them the utilization of Jimson's travellers' cheques. What was to be done? There was a grey area here. But it could wait. It could wait.

At 9.30—8.30 by English time—a reasonable hour to make his call, Kemp picked up the telephone in his room, asked for a line, dialled the code for England, Oxford, and then the number.

The ringing tone went on for longer than he expected before he got through, with Claire on the line.

'Guess who?' he said in a mock-conspiratorial tone, ready with his laughter.

'Ron. God. Is that you? What a surprise. Mike told me you couldn't phone.'

'They don't have any say in the matter,' he said. He laughed triumphantly. 'That's a thing of the past. I'm out of their clutches. I pulled out.'

'Out of Libya, you mean? You've left Libya?'

'I have indeed. Ringing from Tunis.'

'But what are you going to do? Are you going back?' Kemp found her surprisingly—almost alarmingly—matter-of-fact. She clearly hadn't any idea of what he'd been through.

'I'm not going back,' he said. 'Not on your life. I've had Libya, and Libya's had me. Curtains. Finished. I'm not even thinking of the next move at this stage. Probably look round for something in England. Anyway, I'm on my way home. Probably be in tomorrow, in the afternoon. Depending on flights.'

There was a moment of silence while he awaited the joyful outcry. 'Ronald,' she said.

'Yes, what is it?'

'I don't know how to put this, but something's happened.' There was something frightening in the flatness of her voice.

'Something's happened? In what way? Are the boys all right? Something about the house?'

'It's you and me. I don't know how to explain it to you. I wasn't expecting to hear from you. Teddy Vickers is here. I'm going to call him.'

'Wait a minute,' Kemp said, but she had gone, then Vickers was on the line. 'Ron, I can't tell you how badly I feel about this, but what can I say? I quite thought you'd have cottoned on by now. Claire and I—well, there it is. Don't think I'm trying to shift the blame, because I'm not, but you did leave her on her own to cope with things for rather a long while. Actually I fully intended to fly over for a chat with you about the situation. See if there was anything to be done. It got put off. I'm sorry, Ron, and you know I mean that. We're both of us civilized human beings.'

Kemp hung up and settled with his head in his hands, but instantly the buzzer went and the reception was on the line. 'Mr Kemp, we should like to have your passport if that is convenient.'

'My passport? Oh yes.'

Dully, he thought, no date of entry stamp. Have to ring up the Embassy. See if they can issue a new one.

'I'll bring it down later,' he said, 'and by the way I may be staying somewhat longer than I thought. Several days, anyway.'

'Thank you, Mr Kemp. You are welcome. I will mark indefinite stay in the register.'